# T̶ʜᴇ MAGICIAN'S ELEPHANT

# THE MAGICIAN'S ELEPHANT

### KATE DiCAMILLO

*illustrated by* Yoko Tanaka

WALKER
BOOKS

First published 2009 by Walker Books Ltd
87 Vauxhall Walk, London SE11 5HJ

This edition published 2015

2 4 6 8 10 9 7 5 3 1

Text © 2009 Kate DiCamillo
Illustrations © 2009, 2015 Yoko Tanaka

The right of Kate DiCamillo and Yoko Tanaka to be identified as
author and illustrator respectively of this work has been asserted by them
in accordance with the Copyright, Designs and Patents Act 1988

This book has been typeset in LTC Pabst Oldstyle

Printed and bound in Great Britain by Clays Ltd, St Ives plc

British Library Cataloguing in Publication Data:
a catalogue record for this book is available from the British Library

ISBN 978-1-4063-6065-3

www.walker.co.uk

*For H. S. L. and A. M. T.*
*They walked ahead of me.*
*K. D.*


*For Daniel Favini, who magically appeared in*
*my life and made my world blossom.*
*Y. T.*

## Chapter One

At the end of the century before last, in the market square of the city of Baltese, there stood a boy with a hat on his head and a coin in his hand. The boy's name was Peter Augustus Duchene, and the coin that he held did not belong to him but was instead the property of his guardian, an old soldier named Vilna Lutz, who had sent the boy to the market for fish and bread.

That day in the market square, in the midst of the entirely unremarkable and absolutely ordinary stalls of the fishmongers and cloth merchants and bakers and silversmiths, there had appeared, without warning or fanfare, the red tent of a fortune-teller. Attached to the fortune-teller's tent was a piece of paper, and penned upon the paper in a cramped but unapologetic hand were these words:

*The most profound and difficult questions that could possibly be posed by the human mind or heart will be answered within for the price of one florit.*

Peter read the small sign once, and then again. The audacity of the words, their dizzying promise, made it difficult suddenly for him to breathe. He looked down at the coin, the single florit, in his hand.

"But I cannot do it," he said to himself. "Truly, I cannot; for if I do, Vilna Lutz will ask where the money has gone and I will have to lie, and it is a very dishonourable thing to lie."

He put the coin in his pocket. He took the soldier's hat off his head and then put it back on. He stepped away from the sign and came back to it, and stood considering, again, the outrageous and wonderful words.

"But I must know," he said at last. He took the florit from his pocket. "I want to know the truth. And so I will do it. But I will not lie about it, and in that way, I will remain at least partly honourable." With these words, Peter stepped into the tent and handed the fortune-teller the coin.

And she, without even looking at him, said, "One florit will buy you one answer and only one. Do you understand?"

"Yes," said Peter.

He stood in the small patch of light

making its sullen way through the open flap of the tent. He let the fortune-teller take his hand. She examined it closely, moving her eyes back and forth and back and forth, as if there were a whole host of very small words inscribed there, an entire book about Peter Augustus Duchene composed atop his palm.

"Huh," she said at last. She dropped his hand and squinted up at his face. "But, of course, you are just a boy."

"I am ten years old," said Peter. He took the hat from his head and stood as straight and tall as he was able. "And I am training to become a soldier, brave and true. But it does not matter how old I am. You took the florit, so now you must give me my answer."

"A soldier brave and true?" said the fortune-teller. She laughed and spat on the ground. "Very well, soldier brave and true, if you say it is so, then it is so. Ask me your question."

Peter felt a small stab of fear. What if, after all this time, he could not bear the truth? What if he did not really want to know?

"Speak," said the fortune-teller. "Ask."

"My parents," said Peter.

"That is your question?" said the fortune-teller. "They are dead."

Peter's hands trembled. "That is not my question," he said. "I know that already. You must tell me something that I do not know. You must tell me of another — you must tell me..."

The fortune-teller narrowed her eyes. "Ah," she said. "Her? Your sister? That is your question? Very well. She lives."

Peter's heart seized upon the words. *She lives. She lives!*

"No, please," said Peter. He closed his eyes. He concentrated. "If she lives, then I must find her; so my question is, how do I make my way there, to where she is?"

He kept his eyes closed; he waited.

"The elephant," said the fortune-teller.

"What?" Peter said. He opened his eyes, certain that he had misunderstood.

"You must follow the elephant," said the fortune-teller. "She will lead you there."

Peter's heart, which had risen up high inside him, now sank slowly back to its normal resting place. He put his hat on his head. "You are having fun with me," he said. "There are no elephants here."

"Just as you say," said the fortune-teller. "That is surely the truth, at least for now. But perhaps you have not noticed: the truth is forever changing." She winked at him. "Wait awhile," she said. "You will see."

Peter stepped out of the tent. The sky was grey and heavy with clouds, but everywhere people talked and laughed. Vendors shouted and children cried and a beggar with a black dog at his side stood in the centre of it all and sang a song about the darkness.

There was not a single elephant in sight.

Still, Peter's stubborn heart would not be silenced. It beat out the two simple, impossible words over and over again: *She lives, she lives, she lives.*

Could it be?

No, it could not be, for that would mean that Vilna Lutz had lied to him, and it was not at all an honourable thing for a soldier, a superior officer, to lie. Surely Vilna Lutz would not lie. Surely he would not.

Would he?

"It is winter," sang the beggar. "It is dark and cold, and things are not what they seem, and the truth is forever changing."

"I do not know what the truth is," said Peter, "but I do know that I must confess. I must tell Vilna Lutz what I have done." He squared his shoulders, adjusted his hat and began the long walk back to the Apartments Polonaise.

As he walked, the winter afternoon turned to dusk and the grey light gave way to gloom, and Peter thought: The fortune-teller is lying; no, Vilna Lutz is lying; no, it is the fortune-teller who lies; no, no, it is Vilna Lutz ... on and on like that, the whole way back.

And when he came to the Apartments Polonaise, he climbed the stairs to the attic apartment very slowly, putting one foot carefully in front of the other, thinking with each step, He lies; she lies; he lies; she lies.

The old soldier was waiting for him, sitting in a chair at the window, a single candle lit, the papers of a battle plan in his lap, his shadow cast large on the wall behind him.

"You are late, Private Duchene," said Vilna Lutz. "And you are empty-handed."

"Sir," said Peter. He took off his hat. "I have no fish and no bread. I gave the money to a fortune-teller."

"A fortune-teller?" said Vilna Lutz. "A fortune-teller!" He tapped his left foot, the one made of wood, against the floorboards. "A fortune-teller? You must explain yourself."

Peter said nothing.

*Tap, tap, tap,* went Vilna Lutz's wooden foot, *tap, tap, tap.* "I am waiting," he said. "Private Duchene, I am waiting for you to explain."

"It is only that I have doubts, sir," said Peter. "And I know that I should not have doubts—"

"Doubts! Doubts? Explain yourself."

"Sir, I cannot explain myself. I have been trying the whole way here. There is no explanation that will suffice."

"Very well, then," said Vilna Lutz. "You will allow me to explain for you. You have spent money that did not belong to you. You have spent it in a foolish way. You have acted dishonourably. You will be punished. You will retire without your evening rations."

"Sir, yes, sir," said Peter, but he continued to stand, his hat in his hands, in front of Vilna Lutz.

"Is there something else you wish to say?"

"No. Yes."

"Which is it, please? No? Or yes?"

"Sir, have you yourself ever told a lie?" said Peter.

"I?"

"Yes," said Peter. "You. Sir."

Vilna Lutz sat up straighter in his chair. He raised a hand and stroked his beard, tracing the line of it, making certain that the hairs were arranged just so, that they came together in a fine, military point. At last he said, "You who spend money that is not yours — you who spend the money of others like a fool — *you* will speak to *me* of who lies?"

"I am sorry, sir," said Peter.

"I am quite certain that you are," said Vilna Lutz. "You are also dismissed." He picked up his papers. He held the battle plan up to the light of the candle and muttered to himself, "So, and it must be so, and then ... so."

Later that night, when the candle was quenched and the room was in darkness and the old soldier was snoring in his bed, Peter Augustus Duchene lay on his pallet on the floor and looked up at the ceiling and thought, He lies; she lies; he lies; she lies.

Someone lies, but I do not know who.

If *she* lies, with her ridiculous talk of elephants, then I am, as Vilna Lutz said, a fool — a fool who believes that an elephant will appear and lead me to a sister who is dead.

But if *he* lies, then my sister is alive.

His heart thumped.

If he lies, then Adele lives.

"I hope that he lies," said Peter aloud to the darkness.

And his heart, startled at such treachery,

astonished at the voicing aloud of such an unsoldierly sentiment, thumped again, much harder this time.

Not far from the Apartments Polonaise, across the rooftops and through the darkness of the winter night, stood the Bliffendorf Opera House, and that evening upon its stage, a magician of advanced years and failing reputation performed the most astonishing magic of his career.

He intended to conjure a bouquet of lilies, but instead the magician brought forth an elephant.

The elephant came crashing through the ceiling of the opera house amid a shower of plaster dust and roofing tiles and landed in the lap of a noblewoman, a certain Madam Bettine LaVaughn, to whom the magician had intended to present the bouquet.

Madam LaVaughn's legs were crushed. She was thereafter confined to a wheelchair and given to exclaiming often, and in a voice of wonder, in the midst of some conversation that had nothing at all to do with elephants or roofs, "But perhaps you do not understand. I was crippled by an elephant! Crippled by an elephant that came through the roof!"

As for the magician, he was immediately, at the behest of Madam LaVaughn, imprisoned.

The elephant was imprisoned too.

She was locked in a stable. A chain was wrapped around her left ankle. The chain was attached to an iron rod planted firmly in the earth.

At first, the elephant felt one thing and one thing only: dizzy. If she turned her head too quickly to the right or the left, she was aware of the world spinning in a truly alarming manner. So she did not turn her head. She closed her eyes and kept them closed.

There was, all about her, a great hubbub and roar. The elephant ignored it. She wanted nothing more than for the world to hold itself still.

After a few hours, the dizziness passed. The elephant opened her eyes and looked around her and realized that she did not know where she was.

She knew only one thing to be true.

Where she was was not where she should be.

Where she was was not where she belonged.

## Chapter Two

The day after the night that the elephant arrived, Peter was again at the market square. The fortune-teller's tent was gone, and Peter had been entrusted with another florit. The old soldier had talked at great length and in excruciating detail about what Peter had to purchase with the coin. Bread, for one, and it should be bread that was at least a day old, two days old preferably, but three-day-old bread, if he could find it, would be the best of all.

"Actually, see if you cannot locate bread with mould growing on it," said Vilna Lutz. "Old bread is a most excellent preparation for being a soldier. Soldiers must become accustomed to rock-hard bread that is difficult to chew. It makes for strong teeth. And strong teeth make for a strong heart and therefore a brave soldier. Yes, yes, I believe it to be true. I know it to be true."

How hard bread and strong teeth and a strong heart were connected was a mystery to Peter, but as Vilna Lutz spoke to him that morning, it became increasingly obvious that the old soldier was once again in the grip of a fever and that not much sense would be had from him.

"You must ask the fishmonger for two fish and no more," Vilna Lutz said. Sweat shone on his forehead. His beard was damp. "Ask him for the smallest ones. Ask him for the fish that others would turn away. Why, you must ask him for those fish that the other fish are embarrassed even to refer to as fish! Come back with the smallest fish, but do not — do not, I repeat — come back to me empty-handed with the lies of fortune-tellers upon your lips! I correct myself! I correct myself! To say 'the lies of fortune-tellers' is a redundancy. What comes from the mouths of fortune-tellers is by definition a lie; and you, Private Duchene, you must, you *must*, find the smallest possible fish."

So Peter stood in the market square, in line at the fishmonger's, thinking of the fortune-teller and his sister and elephants and fevers and exceptionally small fish. He also thought of lies and who told them and who did not and what it meant to be a soldier, honourable and true. And because of all the thoughts in his head, he was listening with only half an ear to the story that the fishmonger was telling to the woman ahead of him in line.

"Well, he wasn't much of a magician, and none of them was expecting much, you see — that's the thing. Nothing was expected." The fishmonger wiped his hands on his apron. "He hadn't promised them nothing special, and they wasn't expecting it neither."

"Who expects something special nowadays anyway?" said the woman. "Not me. I've worn myself out expecting something special." She pointed to a large fish. "Give me one of them mackerels, why don't you?"

"Mackerel it is," said the fishmonger, slinging the creature onto the scales. It was a very large fish. Vilna Lutz would not have approved.

Peter surveyed the fishmonger's selection. His stomach growled. He was hungry, and he was worried. He could not see anything alarmingly small enough to please the old soldier.

"And also give me catfish," said the woman. "Three of them. I want 'em with the whiskers longish, don't I? Tastier that way."

The fishmonger put three catfish on the scales. "In any case," he continued, "they was all sitting there, the nobility, the ladies and the princes and the princesses, all together in the opera house, expecting nothing much. And what did they get?"

"I don't even pretend to know," said the woman. "What fancy people get is most surely a mystery to me."

Peter shifted nervously from foot to foot. He wondered what would happen to him if he did not bring home a fish that was sufficiently small. There was no predicting what Vilna Lutz would say or do when he was in the grip of one of his terrible recurring fevers.

"Well, they wasn't expecting an elephant — that much is for true."

"An elephant!" said the woman.

"An elephant?" said Peter. At the sound of

the impossible word on the lips of another, he felt a shock travel from the tip of his feet to the top of his head. He stepped backwards.

"An elephant!" said the fishmonger. "Come right through the ceiling of the opera house, landed on top of a noblewoman named LaVaughn."

"An elephant," whispered Peter.

"Ha," said the woman, "ha ha. It most surely couldn't have."

"It did," said the fishmonger. "Broke her legs!"

"La, the humour of it, and don't my friend Marcelle wash the linens of Madam LaVaughn? Ain't the world as small as it can be?"

"Just exactly," said the fishmonger.

"But, please," said Peter, "an elephant. An elephant. Do you know what you say?"

"Yes," said the fishmonger, "I say an elephant."

"And she came through the roof?"

"Didn't I just say that too?"

"Where is this elephant now, please?" said Peter.

"The police have got her," said the fishmonger.

"The police!" said Peter. He put his hand up to his hat. He took the hat off and put it back on and took it off again.

"Is the child having some sort of hat-related fit?" said the woman to the fishmonger.

"It's just as the fortune-teller said," said Peter. "An elephant."

"How's that?" said the fishmonger. "Who said it?"

"It doesn't matter," said Peter. "Nothing matters except that the elephant has come. And what that means."

"And what does it mean?" said the fishmonger. "I would surely like to know."

"That she lives," said Peter. "That she lives."

"And ain't that grand?" said the fishmonger. "We are always happy when people live, ain't we?"

"Sure, and why not?" said the woman. "But what I want to know is what's become of him who started it all? Where's the magician?"

"Imprisoned him," said the fishmonger, "didn't they? Put him in the most terrible cell of all and threw away the key."

The prison cell to which the magician was confined was small and dark. But there was, in the cell, one window, very high up. At night the magician lay atop his cloak on his mattress of straw and looked out of the window into the darkness of the world. The sky was almost always thick with clouds, but sometimes, if the magician stared long enough, the clouds

would grudgingly part and reveal one exceedingly bright star.

"I intended only lilies," the magician said to the star. "That was my intention: a bouquet of lilies."

This was not, strictly speaking, the truth.

Yes, the magician had intended to conjure lilies.

But standing on the stage of the Bliffendorf Opera House, before an audience that was indifferent to whatever small diversion he might perform and was waiting only for him to exit and for the real magic (the music of a virtuoso violinist) to begin, the magician was struck suddenly, and quite forcibly, with the notion that he had wasted his life.

So he performed that night the sleight of hand that would result in lilies, but at the same time, he muttered the words of a spell that his magic teacher had entrusted to him long ago. The magician knew that the words were powerful and also, given the circumstances, somewhat ill-advised. But he wanted to perform something spectacular.

And he had.

That night at the opera house, before the whole world exploded into screams and sirens and accusations, the magician stood next to the enormous beast and gloried in the smell of her — dried apples, mouldy paper, dung. He reached out and placed a hand, one hand, on her chest and felt, for a moment, the solemn beating of her heart.

This, he thought. I did this.

And when he was commanded, later that night, by every authority imaginable (the mayor, a duke, a princess, the chief of police) to send the elephant back, to make her go away — to, in essence, *disappear* her — the magician had dutifully spoken the spell, as well as the words themselves, backwards, as the magic required, but nothing happened. The elephant remained absolutely, emphatically, undeniably *there*, her very presence serving as some indisputable evidence of his powers.

He had intended lilies; yes, perhaps.

But he had also wanted to perform true magic.

He had succeeded.

And so, no matter what words he may have spoken to the star that occasionally appeared above him, the magician could summon no true regret for what he had done.

The star, it should be noted, was not a star at all.

It was the planet Venus.

Records indicate that it shone particularly bright that year.

## Chapter Three

The chief of police of the city of Baltese was a man who believed most firmly in the letter of the law. However, despite repeated and increasingly flustered consultations of the police handbook, he could not find one word, one syllable, one letter, that pertained to the correct method of dealing with a beast that has appeared out of nowhere, destroying the roof of an opera house and crippling a noblewoman.

And so, with great reluctance, the chief of

police solicited the opinions of his subordinates about what should be done with the elephant.

"Sir!" said one of the young sergeants. "She appeared. Perhaps, if we are patient, she will disappear."

"Does the elephant appear as if she might disappear?" said the chief of police.

"Sir?" said the young sergeant. "I am afraid I don't understand the question, sir."

"I am quite aware of your lack of understanding," said the chief. "Your lack of understanding is as apparent as the elephant and is even more unlikely to disappear."

"Yes, sir," said the sergeant. He furrowed his brow. He thought for a moment. "Thank you, sir, I'm sure."

This exchange was followed by a long and painful silence. The gathered policemen shuffled their feet.

"It is simple," said another policeman finally. "The elephant is a criminal. Therefore she must be tried as a criminal and punished as a criminal."

"But why is the elephant a criminal?" said a small policeman with a very large moustache.

"Why is the elephant a criminal?" said the police chief.

"Yes," said the small policeman, whose name was Leo Matienne, "why? If the magician threw a rock at a window, would you then blame the rock for the window breaking?"

"What kind of magician throws rocks?" said the chief of police. "What kind of sorry excuse for magic is that, the throwing of rocks?"

"You misunderstand me, sir," said Leo Matienne. "I meant only to say that the elephant did not ask to come crashing through the roof of the opera house. Would any sensible elephant wish for such a thing? And if she did not wish for it, then how can she be guilty of it?"

"I ask you for possible solutions," said the chief of police. He put his hands on top of his head.

"Yes," said Leo Matienne.

"I ask what action should be taken," said the chief. He pulled at his hair with both hands.

"Yes," said Leo Matienne again.

"And you talk to me about sensible elephants and what they wish for?" shouted the captain.

"I think it is pertinent, sir," said Leo Matienne.

"He thinks it is pertinent," said the chief. "He thinks it is pertinent." He pulled at his hair again. His face became very red.

"Sir," said another policeman, "what if we found the elephant a home, sir?"

"Yes," said the chief of police. He turned around and faced the policeman who had just spoken. "Why did I not think of it? Let us dispatch the elephant immediately to the Home for Wayward Elephants Who Engage in Objectionable Pursuits Against Their Will. It is right down the street, is it not?"

"Is it?" said the policeman. "Truly? I had not known. There are so many worthy charitable institutions in this enlightened age; why, it's become nearly impossible to keep track of them all."

The chief pulled very hard at his hair. "Leave me," he said softly. "All of you. I will solve this without your help."

One by one, the policemen left the police station.

The small policeman was the last to go. He lifted his hat to the chief.

"I wish you a good evening, sir," he said, "and I beg that you consider the idea that the elephant is guilty of nothing except being an elephant."

"Leave me," said the chief of police, "please."

"Good evening, sir," said Leo Matienne again. "Good evening."

The small policeman walked home in the gloom of early evening. As he walked, he whistled a sad song and considered the fate of the elephant.

To his mind, the chief was asking the wrong questions.

The questions that mattered, the questions that needed to be asked, were these: where did the elephant come from? And what did it mean that she had come to the city of Baltese?

What if she was just the first in a series of elephants? What if, one by one, all the mammals and reptiles of Africa were to be summoned to the stages of opera houses all across Europe?

What if, next, crocodiles and giraffes and

rhinoceroses came crashing through roofs?

Leo Matienne had the soul of a poet, and because of this, he liked very much to consider questions that had no answers.

He liked to ask "What if?" and "Why not?" and "Could it possibly be?"

Leo came to the top of the hill and paused. Below him the lamplighter was lighting the lamps that lined the wide avenue. Leo Matienne stood and watched as, one by one, the globes sprang to life.

What if the elephant had come bearing a message of great importance?

What if everything was to be irrevocably, undeniably changed by the elephant's arrival?

Leo stood at the top of the hill and waited for a long while, until the avenue below him was well and fully lit, and then he continued walking down the hill and onto the lighted path, towards his home.

He whistled as he walked.

*What if? Why not? Could it be?* sang the glowing, wondering heart of Leo Matienne.

What if?

Why not?

Could it be?

Peter stood at the window of the attic room of the Apartments Polonaise. He heard Leo Matienne before he saw him; always, because of the whistling, Peter heard Leo before he saw him.

He waited until the policeman appeared, and then he threw open the window and stuck his head out. He shouted, "Leo Matienne, is it true that there is an elephant and that she came through the roof and that she is now with the police?"

Leo stopped. He looked up.

"Peter," he said. He smiled. "Peter Augustus Duchene, fellow resident of the Apartments Polonaise, little cuckoo bird of the attic world. There is indeed an elephant. It is true. And it is true, also, that she is in the custody of the police. The elephant is imprisoned."

"Where?" said Peter.

"I cannot say," said Leo Matienne. "I cannot say, because I am afraid that I do not know. They are keeping it the strictest possible secret, you see, what with elephants being such dangerous and provoking criminals."

"Close the window," called Vilna Lutz from his bed. "It is winter, and it is cold."

It was winter, true.

And true, also, it was quite cold.

But even in the summertime, Vilna Lutz, when he was in the grip of his strange fever, would complain of the cold and demand that the window be shut.

"Thank you," said Peter to Leo Matienne. He closed the window and turned and faced the old man.

"What were you speaking of?" said Vilna Lutz. "What manner of nonsense were you shouting from windows?"

"An elephant, sir," said Peter. "It is true. Leo Matienne says that it is true. An elephant has arrived. An elephant is here."

"Elephants," said Vilna Lutz. "Pooh. Imaginary beasts, denizens of bestiaries, demons from who knows where." He fell back against the pillow, exhausted by his diatribe, and then jerked suddenly upright again. "Hark! Do I hear the crack of muskets, the boom of cannon?"

"No, sir," said Peter. "You do not."

"Demons, elephants, imaginary beasts."

"Not imaginary," said Peter. "Real. This elephant is real. Leo Matienne is an officer of the law, and he says that it is so."

"Pooh," said Vilna Lutz. "I say 'pooh' to that mustachioed officer of the law and his imagined creature." He lay back against the pillow. He turned his head first to one side and then to the other. "I hear it," he said. "I hear the sounds of battle. The fight has begun."

"So," said Peter softly to himself, "it must be true, mustn't it? There is an elephant now, so the fortune-teller was right, and my sister lives."

"Your sister?" said Vilna Lutz. "Your sister is dead. How often must I tell you? She never drew breath. She did not breathe. They are all dead. Look out over the field and you will see: they are all dead, your father among them. Look, look! Your father lies dead."

"I see," said Peter.

"Where is my foot?" said Vilna Lutz. He cast a wild look around the room. "Where is it?"

"On the bedside table."

"On the bedside table, *sir*," corrected Vilna Lutz.

"On the bedside table, sir," said Peter.

"There," said the old soldier. He picked up the foot. "There, there, old friend." He gave the wooden foot a loving pat and then let his head sink back on the pillow. He pulled the blankets up under his chin. "Soon," he said, "soon, I will put on the foot, Private Duchene, and we will practise manoeuvres, you and I. We will make a great soldier out of you yet. You will become a man like your father. You will become, like him, a soldier brave and true."

Peter turned away from Vilna Lutz and looked out of the window at the darkening world. Downstairs, far below, a door slammed. And then another. He heard the muffled sound of laughter and knew that Leo Matienne was being welcomed home by his wife.

What was it like, Peter wondered, to have someone who knew you would always return and who welcomed you with open arms?

He remembered being in a garden at dusk. The sky was purple and the lamps had been lit, and Peter was small. His father picked him up and tossed him high and then caught him, over and over again. Peter's mother was there too; she was wearing a white dress that glowed bright in the purple dusk, and her stomach was large like a balloon.

"Don't drop him," said Peter's mother to his father. "Don't you dare drop him." She was laughing.

"I will not," said his father. "I could not. For he is Peter Augustus Duchene, and he will always return to me."

Again and again, Peter's father threw him up in the air. Again and again, Peter felt himself suspended in nothingness for a moment, just a moment, and then he was pulled back, returned to the sweetness of the earth and the warmth of his father's waiting arms.

"See?" said his father to his mother. "Do you see how he always comes back to me?"

It was fully dark now in the attic room of

the Apartments Polonaise. The old soldier tossed from side to side in the bed. "Close the window," he said. "It is winter, and it is cold."

The garden that held Peter's father and mother seemed far away, so far that he could almost believe that the memory, the garden, had existed in another world entirely.

But if the fortune-teller was to be believed (and she must be believed; she must, he thought), the elephant knew the way to that garden. She could lead him there.

"Please," said Vilna Lutz, "the window must be closed. It is so cold; it is so very, very cold."

## Chapter Four

That winter, the winter of the elephant, was, for the city of Baltese, a particularly miserable season. The skies were filled with thick, lowering clouds that obscured the sun and condemned the city to a series of days that resembled nothing so much as a single, unending dusk.

It was unimaginably, unbelievably cold.

Darkness prevailed.

*  *  *

The crippled Madam LaVaughn, sunk deep in a gloom of her own, took to visiting the prison.

She came in the late afternoon.

The magician could hear the accusing creak of the wheels of her chair as it was pushed down the long corridor. Yet, when the noblewoman appeared before him, her eyes wide and pleading, a blanket thrown over her useless legs and her manservant standing to attention behind her, the magician managed, somehow, each time, to be astonished at her presence.

Madam LaVaughn spoke to the magician. She said, "But perhaps you do not understand. I was crippled, crippled by an elephant that came through the roof!"

The magician responded. He said, "Madam LaVaughn, I assure you, I intended only lilies. I intended only a bouquet of lilies."

Every day, the magician and the noblewoman spoke to each other with an urgency

that belied the fact that they had spoken the same words the day before and the day before that.

Every afternoon, the magician and Madam LaVaughn faced each other in the gloom of the prison and said exactly the same thing.

The noblewoman's manservant was named Hans Ickman, and he had been in the service of Madam LaVaughn since she was a child. He was her adviser and confidant, and she trusted him in all things.

Before he came to serve Madam LaVaughn, however, Hans Ickman had lived in a small town in the mountains, and he had had there a family: brothers, a mother and a father, and a dog who was famous for being able to leap across the river that ran through the woods beyond the town.

The river was too wide for Hans Ickman

and his brothers to leap across. It was too wide even for a grown man to leap. But the dog would take a running jump and sail effortlessly across the water. She was a white dog and small, and other than her ability to jump the river, she was in no way extraordinary.

Hans Ickman, as he aged, had forgotten about the dog entirely; her miraculous ability had receded to the back of his mind. But the night that the elephant had come crashing through the ceiling of the opera house, the manservant had remembered again, for the first time in a long while, the little white dog.

Standing in the prison, listening to the endless and unvarying exchange between Madam LaVaughn and the magician, Hans Ickman thought about being a boy, waiting on the bank of the river with his brothers, and watching the dog run and then fling herself into the air. He remembered how, in mid-leap, she would always twist her body, a small unnecessary gesture, a fillip of joy, to show that this impossible thing was easy for her.

Madam LaVaughn said, "But perhaps you do not understand."

The magician said, "I intended only lilies."

Hans Ickman closed his eyes and remembered the dog suspended in the air above the river, her white body set afire by the light of the sun.

But what was the dog's name? He could not recall. She was gone and her name was gone with her. Life was so short; so many beautiful things slipped away. Where, for instance, were his brothers now? He did not know; he could not say.

Madam LaVaughn said, "I was crushed, crushed by an elephant!"

The magician said, "I intended only—"

"Please," said Hans Ickman. He opened

his eyes. "It is important that you say what you mean to say. Time is too short. You must speak words that matter."

The magician and the noblewoman were silent for a moment.

And then Madam LaVaughn opened her mouth. She said, "But perhaps you do not understand."

The magician said, "I intended only lilies."

"Enough," said Hans Ickman. He took hold of Madam LaVaughn's chair and turned it around. "That is enough. I cannot bear to hear it any more. I truly cannot."

He wheeled her away, down the long corridor and out of the prison and into the cold, dark Baltesian afternoon.

"But perhaps you do not understand. I was crippled—"

"No," said Hans Ickman, "no."

Madam LaVaughn fell silent.

And it was in this manner that she paid her last official visit to the magician in prison.

Peter could, from the window of the attic room in the Apartments Polonaise, see the turrets of the prison. He could see, too, the spire of the city's largest cathedral and the gargoyles crouched there, glowering, on its ledges. If he looked out into the distance, he could see the great, grand homes of the nobility high atop the hill. Below him were the twisting, turning cobblestoned streets, the small shops with their crooked tiled roofs, and the pigeons who forever perched atop them, singing sad songs that did not quite begin and never truly ended.

It was a terrible thing to gaze upon it all and know that somewhere, beneath one of those roofs, hidden, perhaps, in some dark alley, was the very thing that he needed, wanted, and could not have.

How could it be that against all odds, all expectations, all reason, an elephant could miraculously appear in the city of Baltese and then just as quickly disappear; and that he, Peter Augustus Duchene, who needed desperately to find her, did not know — could not even begin to imagine — the how or where of searching for her?

Looking out over the city, Peter decided that it was a terrible and complicated thing to hope, and that it might be easier, instead, to despair.

"Come away from the window," Vilna Lutz called to Peter.

Peter held very still. He found that it was hard now for him to look at Vilna Lutz's face.

"Private Duchene," said Vilna Lutz.

"Sir?" said Peter without turning.

"A battle is being waged," said Vilna Lutz, "a battle between good and evil! Whose side will you do battle on? Private Duchene!"

Peter turned and faced the old man.

"What is this? Are you crying?"

"No," said Peter. "I am not." But when he put a hand to his face, he was surprised to discover that his cheek was wet.

"That is good," said Vilna Lutz. "Soldiers do not weep; at least, they should not weep. It is not to be borne, the weeping of soldiers. Something is amiss in the universe when a soldier cries. Hark! Do you hear the rattle of muskets?"

"I do not," said Peter.

"Oh, it is cold," said the old soldier. "Still, we must practise manoeuvres. The marching must begin. Yes, the marching must begin."

Peter did not move.

"Private Duchene! You will march! Armies must move. Soldiers must march."

Peter sighed. His heart was so heavy inside him that he did not, in truth, think that he had it in him to move at all. He lifted one foot and then the other.

"Higher," said Vilna Lutz. "March with purpose; march like a man. March as your father would have marched."

What difference does it make if an elephant has come? Peter thought as he stood in the same place and marched without going anywhere at all. It is just some grand and terrible joke that the fortune-teller has told me. My sister is not alive. There is no reason to hope.

The longer he marched, the more convinced Peter became that things were indeed hopeless and that an elephant was a ridiculous answer to any question — but a particularly ridiculous answer to a question posed by the human heart.

## Chapter Five

The people of the city of Baltese became obsessed with the elephant.

In the market square and in the ballrooms, in the stables and in the gaming houses, in the churches and in the squares, it was "the elephant", "the elephant that came through the roof", "the elephant conjured by the magician", "the elephant that crippled the noblewoman".

The bakers of the city concocted a flat, oversized pastry and filled it with cream and sprinkled it with cinnamon and sugar and called the confection an elephant ear, and the people could not get enough of it.

The street vendors sold, for exorbitant prices, chunks of plaster that had fallen onto the stage when the elephant made her dramatic appearance. "Cataclysm!" the vendors shouted. "Mayhem! Possess the plaster of disaster!"

The puppet shows in the public gardens featured elephants that came crashing onto the stage, crushing the other puppets beneath them, making the young children laugh and clap in delight and recognition.

From the pulpits of the churches the preachers spoke about divine intervention, the surprises of fate, the wages of sin, and the dire consequences of magic gone afoul.

The elephant's dramatic and unexpected appearance changed the way the people of the city of Baltese spoke. If, for instance, a person was deeply surprised or moved, he or she would say, "I was, you understand, in the presence of the elephant."

As for the fortune-tellers of the city, they were kept particularly busy. They gazed into their teacups and crystal balls. They read the palms of thousands of hands. They studied their cards and cleared their throats and predicted that amazing things were yet to come. If elephants could arrive without warning, then a dramatic shift had certainly occurred in the universe. The stars were aligning themselves for something even more spectacular; rest assured, rest assured.

Meanwhile, in the dance halls and in the ballrooms, the men and the women of the city, the low and the high, danced the same dance: a swaying, lumbering two-step called, of course, the Elephant.

Everywhere, always, it was "the elephant, the elephant, the magician's elephant".

*  *  *

"It is absolutely ruining the social season," said the Countess Quintet to her husband. "It is all people will speak of. Why, it is as bad as a war. Actually, it is worse. At least with a war, there are well-dressed heroes capable of making interesting conversation. But what do we have here? Nothing, nothing but a smelly, loathsome beast, and yet people *will* insist on speaking of nothing else. I truly feel, I am quite certain, I am absolutely convinced, that I will lose my mind if I hear the word *elephant* one more time.

"Elephant," muttered the count.

"What did you say?" said the countess. She whirled around and stared at her husband.

"Nothing," said the count.

"Something must be done," said the countess.

"Indeed," said Count Quintet, "and who will do it?"

"I beg your pardon?"

The count cleared his throat. "I only wanted to say, my dear, that you must admit that what occurred was indeed truly extraordinary."

"Why must I admit it? What was extraordinary about it?"

The countess had not been present at the opera house that fateful evening, and so she had missed the cataclysmic event; and the countess was the kind of person who hated, most horribly, to miss cataclysmic events.

"Well, you see—" began Count Quintet.

"I do not see," said the countess. "And you will not make me see."

"Yes," said her husband, "I suppose that much is true."

Unlike his wife, the count had been in attendance at the opera house that night. He had been seated so close to the stage that he had felt the rush of displaced air that presaged the elephant's appearance.

"There must be a way to wrest control of the situation," said the Countess Quintet. She paced back and forth. "There must be some way to regain the social season."

The count closed his eyes. He felt again the breeze of the elephant's arrival. The whole thing had happened in an instant, but it had also occurred so slowly. He, who never cried, had cried that night, because it was as if the elephant had spoken to him and said, "Things are not at all what they seem to be; oh no, not at all."

To be in the presence of such a thing, to feel such a feeling!

Count Quintet opened his eyes.

"My dear," he said, "I have the solution."

"You do?" said the countess.

"Yes."

"And what, exactly, would the solution be?"

"If everyone speaks of nothing but the elephant, and if you desire to be the centre, the heart, of the social season, then you must be the one with the thing that everyone speaks of."

"But what can you mean?" said the countess. Her lower lip quivered. "Whatever can you mean?"

"What I mean, my dear, is that you must bring the magician's elephant here."

When the countess demanded of the universe that it move in a certain way, the universe, trembling and eager to please, did as she bade it do.

And so, in the matter of the elephant and the countess, this is how it happened — this is how it unfolded. There was not, at her home, as lavish and well appointed a home as it was, a door large enough for an elephant to walk through. The Countess Quintet hired a dozen craftsmen. The men worked around the clock, and within a day a wall had been knocked down and an enormous, brightly painted, handsomely decorated door installed.

The elephant was summoned and arrived under cover of night, escorted by the chief of police, who ushered her through the door that had been constructed expressly for her; then, relieved beyond all measure to have done with the affair, he tipped his hat to the countess and left.

The door was closed and locked behind him, and the elephant became the property of the Countess Quintet, who had paid the owner of the opera house money sufficient to repair and retile the whole of his roof a dozen times over.

The elephant belonged entirely to the Countess Quintet, who had written to Madam LaVaughn and expressed at great length and with the utmost eloquence her sorrow over the unspeakable and inexplicable tragedy that had befallen the noblewoman; she offered Madam

LaVaughn her full and enthusiastic support in the further prosecution and punishment of the magician.

The fate of the elephant rested absolutely in the hands of the Countess Quintet, who had made a very generous contribution indeed to the policemen's fund.

The elephant, you will now understand, belonged lock, stock and barrel to the countess.

The beast was installed in the ballroom, and the ladies and gentlemen, dukes and duchesses, princes and princesses, and counts and countesses flocked to her.

They gathered around her.

The elephant became, quite literally, the centre of the social season.

## Chapter Six

Peter dreamed.

Vilna Lutz was ahead of him in a field, and he, Peter, was running to catch up.

"Hurry!" shouted Vilna Lutz. "You must run like a soldier."

The field was a field of wheat, and as Peter ran, the wheat grew taller and taller, and soon it was so tall that Vilna Lutz disappeared entirely from view and Peter could only hear his voice shouting, "Hurry, hurry! Run like a man; run like a soldier!"

"It is no good," said Peter. "No good at all. I have lost him. I will never catch him, and it is pointless to run."

He sat down and looked up at the blue sky. Around him the wheat continued to grow, forming a golden wall, sealing him in, protecting him. It is almost like being buried, he thought. I will stay here for ever, for all time. No one will ever find me.

"Yes," he said, "I will stay here."

And it was then that he noticed that there was a door in the wall of wheat.

Peter stood and went to the wooden door and knocked on it, and the door swung open.

"Hello?" called Peter.

No one answered him.

"Hello?" he called again.

And when there was still no answer, he pushed the door open further and stepped over the threshold and entered the home he had once shared with his mother and father.

Someone was crying.

He went into the bedroom, and there on the bed, wrapped in a blanket, alone and wailing, was a baby.

"Whose baby is this?" Peter said. "Please, whose baby is this?"

The baby continued to cry, and the sound of it was heartbreaking to him, so he bent and picked her up.

"Oh," he said. "Shh. There, there."

He held the baby and rocked her back and forth. After a time, she stopped crying and fell asleep. Peter could not get over how small she was, how easy it was to hold her, how comfortably she fitted in his arms.

The door to the apartment stood open, and he could hear the music of the wind moving through the grain. He looked out of the window and saw the evening sun hanging golden over the field.

For as far as his eye could see, there was nothing but light.

And he knew, suddenly and absolutely, that the baby he held in his arms was his sister, Adele.

When he woke from this dream, Peter sat up straight and looked around the dark room and said, "But that is how it was. She *did* cry. I remember. I held her. And she cried. So she could not, after all, have been born dead and without ever drawing breath, as Vilna Lutz has said time and time again. She cried. You must live to cry."

He lay back down and imagined the weight of his sister in his arms.

Yes, he thought. She cried. I held her. I told my mother that I would watch out for her always. That is how it happened. I know it to be true.

He closed his eyes, and again he saw the door from his dream and felt what it was like to be inside that apartment and to hold his sister and look out at the field of light.

The dream was too beautiful to doubt.

The fortune-teller had not lied.

And if she had not lied about his sister, then perhaps she had told the truth about the elephant too.

"The elephant," said Peter.

He spoke the words aloud to the ever-present dark, to the snoring Vilna Lutz, to the whole of the sleeping and indifferent city of Baltese. "The elephant is what matters. She is with the countess. I must find some way to see her. I will ask Leo Matienne. He is an officer of the law, and he will know what to do. Surely there is some way to get inside, to get to the countess and then to the elephant so that it can all be undone, so that it can at last be put right; because Adele does live. She lives."

Less than five streets from the Apartments Polonaise stood a grim, dark building that bore the somewhat improbable name of the Orphanage of the Sisters of Perpetual Light, and on the top floor of that building was an austere dormitory with a series of small iron beds lined up side by side, one right after the other like metal soldiers. In each of these beds slept an orphan, and the last of the beds in the draughty, overlarge dormitory was occupied by a small girl named Adele, who, soon after the incident at the opera house, began to dream of the magician's elephant.

In Adele's dreams the elephant came and knocked at the door of the orphanage. Sister Marie (the Sister of the Door, the nun who admitted unwanted children to the orphanage and the only person ever allowed to open

and close the front door of the Orphanage of the Sisters of Perpetual Light) was, of course, the one who answered the elephant's knock.

"Good of the evening to you," said the elephant, inclining her head towards Sister Marie. "I have come for the collection of the little person that you are calling by the name Adele."

"Pardon?" said Sister Marie.

"Adele," said the elephant. "I have come for the collection of her. She is belonging elsewhere besides."

"You must speak up," said Sister Marie. "I am old, and I do not hear well."

"It is the one you are calling Adele," said the elephant in a slightly louder voice. "I am coming for to keep her and for taking her to where she is, after all, belonged."

"I am truly sorry," said Sister Marie, and her face did look sad. "I cannot understand a word you are saying. Perhaps it is because you are an elephant? Could that be it? Could that be the cause of the hindrance in our communications? Understand, I have nothing against elephants. You yourself are an exceptionally elegant elephant and obviously well mannered; there is no doubt. But the fact remains that I can make no sense of your words, and so I must bid you goodnight."

And with this, Sister Marie closed the door.

From a window in the dormitory, Adele watched the elephant walk away.

"Madam Elephant!" she shouted, banging on the window. "Here I am. Here! I am Adele. I am the one you are looking for."

But the elephant continued to walk away from her. She went down the street and became smaller and then smaller still, until, in the peculiar and frustrating sleight of hand that often occurs in dreams, the elephant was transformed into a mouse that then scurried into the gutter and disappeared entirely from Adele's view. And then it began to snow.

The cobblestones of the streets and the tiles of the roofs became coated in white. It snowed and snowed until everything disappeared. The world itself soon seemed to cease to exist, erased, bit by bit, by the white of the falling snow.

In the end, there was nothing and no one in the world except for Adele, who stood alone at the window of her dream, waiting.

## Chapter Seven

The city of Baltese felt as if it were under siege — not by a foreign army, but by the weather.

No one could recall a winter so thoroughly, uniformly grey.

Where was the sun?

Would it never shine again?

And if the sun was not going to shine, then could it not at least snow?

Something, anything!

And truly, in the grip of a winter so foul and dark, was it fair to keep a creature as strange and lovely and promising as the elephant locked away from the great majority of the city's people?

It was not fair.

It was not fair at all.

More than a few of the ordinary citizens of Baltese took it upon themselves to knock at the elephant door. When no one answered the knock, they went as far as to try to open the door themselves, but it was locked tight, bolted firm.

"You stay out there," the door seemed to say. "And what is inside here will stay inside here."

And this, in a world so cold and grey, seemed terribly unfair.

Longing is not always a reciprocal thing; while the citizens of Baltese may have longed for the elephant, she did not at all long for them, and finding herself in the ballroom of the countess was, for her, a terrible turn of events.

The glitter of the chandeliers, the thrum of the orchestra, the loud laughter, the smells of roasted meat and cigar smoke and face powder all provoked in her an agony of disbelief.

She tried to will it away. She closed her eyes and kept them closed for as long as she was able, but it made no difference; for whenever she opened them again, it was all as it had been. Nothing had changed.

The elephant felt a terrible pain in her chest.

It was hard for her to breathe; the world seemed too small.

The Countess Quintet, after considerable and extremely careful consultation with her worried advisers, decided that the people of the city (that is, those people who were not invited to her balls and dinners and soirées) could, for their edification and entertainment (and as a way to appreciate the countess's finely tuned sense of social justice), view the elephant for free, absolutely for free, on the first Saturday of the month.

The countess had posters and leaflets printed up and distributed throughout the city, and Leo Matienne, walking home from the police station, stopped to read how he, too, thanks to the largesse of the countess, could see the amazing wonder that was her elephant.

"Ah, thank you very much, Countess," said Leo to the poster. "This is wonderful news, wonderful news indeed."

A beggar stood in the doorway, a black dog at his side, and as soon as Leo Matienne spoke the words, the beggar took them and turned them into a song.

"This is wonderful news," sang the beggar, "wonderful news indeed."

Leo Matienne smiled. "Yes," he said, "wonderful news. I know a young boy who wants quite desperately to see the elephant. He has asked me to assist him, and I have been trying to imagine a way that it could all happen — and now here is the answer before me. He will be so glad of it."

"A boy who wants very much to see the elephant," sang the beggar, "and he will be glad." He stretched out his hand as he sang.

Leo Matienne put a coin in the beggar's hand and bowed before him, and then continued on his walk home, moving more quickly now, whistling the song the beggar had sung and thinking, What if the Countess Quintet becomes weary of the novelty of owning an elephant?

What then?

What if the elephant remembers that she is a creature of the wild and acts accordingly?

What then?

When Leo came at last to the Apartments Polonaise, he heard the creak of the attic window being opened. He looked up and saw Peter's hopeful face staring down at him.

"Please," said Peter, "Leo Matienne, have you figured out a way for the countess to receive me?"

"Peter!" he said. "Little cuckoo bird of the attic world. You are just the person I want to see. But wait; where is your hat?"

"My hat?" said Peter.

"Yes, I have brought you some excellent news, and it seems to me that you would want to have your hat upon your head in order to hear it properly."

"One moment," said Peter. He disappeared from the window and came back again, his hat firmly upon his head.

"And now, then, you are officially attired and ready to receive the happy news of which

I, Leo Matienne, am the proud bearer." Leo cleared his throat. "I am pleased to let you know that the magician's elephant will be on display for the edification and illumination of the masses."

"But what does that mean?" said Peter.

"It means that you may see the elephant on the first Saturday of the month; that is, you may see her this Saturday, Peter, this Saturday."

"Oh," said Peter, "I will see her. I will find her!" His face suddenly became bright, so bright that Leo Matienne, even though he knew it was foolish, turned and checked to see if the sun had somehow performed the impossible and come out from behind a cloud to shine directly on Peter's small face.

There was, of course, no sun.

"Close the window," came the old soldier's voice from inside the attic. "It is winter, and it is cold."

"Thank you," said Peter to Leo Matienne. "Thank you." And he pulled the window shut.

In the apartment of Leo and Gloria Matienne, Leo sat down in front of the fire and heaved a great sigh and took off his boots.

"Phew," said his wife. "Hand me your socks immediately."

Leo removed his socks. Gloria Matienne took them from him and put them directly into a bucket filled with soapy water. "Without me," she said, "you would have no friends at all, because no one would be able to bear the smell of your feet."

"I do not want to surprise you," said Leo, "but, as a matter of course, I keep my boots on in public places and there is no need then for anyone to smell my socks or my feet."

Gloria came up behind Leo and put her hands on his shoulders. She bent and kissed

the top of his head. "What are you thinking?" she said.

"I am imagining Peter," said Leo Matienne, "and how happy he was to learn that he could see the elephant for himself. His face lit up in a way that I have never seen."

"It is wrong about that boy," said Gloria. She sighed. "He is kept a prisoner up there by that man, whatever he is called."

"He is called Lutz," said Leo. "His name is Vilna Lutz."

"All day it is nothing but drilling and marching and more marching. I hear them, you know. It is a terrible sound, terrible."

Leo Matienne shook his head. "It is a terrible thing altogether. He is a gentle boy and not really cut out for soldiering, I do not think. There is a lot of love in him, a lot of love in his heart."

"Most certainly there is," said Gloria.

"And he is up there with no one and

nothing to love. It is a bad thing to have love and nowhere to put it." Leo Matienne sighed. He bent his head back and looked up into his wife's face and smiled. "And we are all alone down here."

"Don't say it," said Gloria Matienne.

"It is only that—"

"No," said Gloria. "No." She put a finger to Leo's lips. "We have tried and failed. God does not intend for us to have children."

"Who are we to say what God intends?" said Leo Matienne. He was silent for a long moment. "What if?"

"Don't you dare," said Gloria. "My heart has been broken too many times, and it cannot bear to hear your foolish questions."

But Leo Matienne would not be silenced. "What if?" he whispered to his wife.

"No," said Gloria.

"Why not?"

"No."

"Could it be?"

"No," said Gloria Matienne, "it cannot be."

## Chapter Eight

At the Orphanage of the Sisters of Perpetual Light, in the cavernous dorm room, in her small bed, Adele was dreaming again of the elephant knocking and knocking, but this time Sister Marie was not at her post, and no one at all came to open the door.

Adele awoke and lay quietly and told herself that it was just a dream, only a dream. But every time she closed her eyes, she saw again the elephant, knocking, knocking, knocking, and no one at all answering her knock. And so she threw back the blanket and got out of bed and went down the stairs in the cold and the dark and made her way to the front door. She was relieved to see that there, just as always, just as for ever, sat Sister Marie in her chair, her head bent so far forward that it rested almost on her stomach, her shoulders rising and falling, and a small sound, something very much like a snore, issuing forth from her mouth.

"Sister Marie," said Adele. She put her hand on the nun's shoulder.

Sister Marie jumped. "But the door is unlocked!" she shouted. "The door is forever unlocked. You must simply knock!"

"I am inside already," said Adele.

"Oh," said Sister Marie, "so you are. So you are. It is you. Adele. How wonderful. Although of course you should not be here.

It is the middle of the night. You should be in your bed."

"I dreamed," said Adele.

"But how lovely," said Sister Marie. "And what did you dream of?"

"The elephant."

"Oh, elephant dreams, yes. I find elephant dreams particularly moving," said Sister Marie, "and portentous, yes, although I am forced to admit that I myself have yet to dream of an elephant. But I wait and hope. One must wait and hope."

"The elephant came here and knocked, and there was no one to answer the door," said Adele.

"But that cannot be," said Sister Marie. "I am always here."

"And then, another night, I dreamed that you opened the door and the elephant was there, and she asked for me and you would not let her in."

"Nonsense," said Sister Marie. "I turn no one away."

"You said you could not understand her."

"I understand how to open a door," said Sister Marie gently. "I did it for you."

Adele sat down on the floor next to Sister Marie's chair. She pulled her knees up to her chest. "What was I like then?" she said. "When I first came here to you."

"Oh, so small, like a mote of dust. You were only a few hours old. You had just been born, you see."

"Were you glad?" said Adele. "Were you glad that I came?" She knew the answer. But she asked anyway.

"I will tell you," said Sister Marie, "that before you arrived, I was sitting here in this chair, alone, and the world was dark, very dark. And then suddenly you were in my arms, and I looked down at you..."

"And you said my name," said Adele.

"Yes, I spoke your name."

"And how did you know it? How did you know my name?"

"The midwife said that your mother, before she died, had insisted that you be called Adele. I knew your name, and I spoke it to you."

"And I smiled," said Adele.

"Yes," said Sister Marie. "And suddenly it seemed that there was light everywhere. The world was filled with light."

Sister Marie's words settled down over Adele like a warm and familiar blanket, and she closed her eyes. "Do you think," she said, "that elephants have names?"

"Oh, yes," said Sister Marie. "All of God's creatures have names, every last one of them. Of that I am sure; of that I have no doubt at all."

Sister Marie was right, of course: everyone has a name.

Beggars have names.

Outside the Orphanage of the Sisters of Perpetual Light, in a narrow alley off a narrow street, sat a beggar named Tomas; huddled up close to him, in an effort both to give and to receive warmth, was a large black dog.

If Tomas had ever had a last name, he did not know it. If he had ever had a mother or a father, he did not know that either.

He knew only that he was a beggar.

He knew how to stretch out his hand and ask.

Also he knew, without knowing how he knew, how to sing.

He knew how to construct a song out of the nothing of day-to-day life and how to sing that nothing into a song so beautiful that it could sustain the vision of a whole and better world.

The dog's name was Iddo.

And there was a time when he had worked carrying messages and letters and plans across

battlefields, transferring information from one officer of Her Majesty's army to another.

And then one day, on a battlefield near Modegnel, as the dog weaved his way through the horses and soldiers and tents, he was caught by the blast from a cannon and was thrown high into the air and landed on his head in such a way that he was instantly, permanently blinded.

His one thought as he descended into darkness was, But who will deliver the messages?

Now when he slept, Iddo was forever running, carrying a letter, a map, battle plans, some piece of paper that would win the war, if only he could arrive with it in time.

The dog longed with the whole of his being to perform again the task that he had been born and bred to do.

Iddo wanted to deliver, just once more, a message of great importance.

In the cold and dark of the alley Iddo whimpered, and Tomas put his hand on the dog's head and kept it there.

"Shh," sang Tomas. "Sleep, Iddo. Darkness falls, but a boy wants to see the elephant; and he will. And this — this — is wonderful news."

Beyond the alley, past the public parks and the police station, up a steep and tree-lined hill, stood the home of the Count and Countess Quintet, and in that mansion, in the darkened ballroom, stood the elephant.

She should have been sleeping, but she was awake.

The elephant was saying her name to herself.

It was not a name that would have made any sense to humans. It was an elephant name — a name that her brothers and sisters knew her by, a name that they spoke in laughter and in play. It was the name that her mother had given to her and that she had spoken often and with love.

Deep within herself, the elephant said this name, her name, over and over again.

She was working to remind herself of who she was. She was working to remember that somewhere, in another place entirely, she was known and loved.

## Chapter Nine

Vilna Lutz's fever receded, and his words began again to make a dull and unremarkable and decidedly military sense. He had risen from his bed and trimmed his beard to a fine point and was seated on the floor. He was placing a collection of lead soldiers in the pattern of a famous battle.

"As you can see, Private Duchene, this was a particularly brilliant strategy on the part of General Von Flickenhamenger, and he executed it with a great deal of grace and bravery, bringing these soldiers from here to here, thereby performing a flanking manoeuvre that was entirely unexpected and exceedingly elegant and devastating. One cannot help but admire the genius of it. Do you admire it, Private Duchene?"

"Yes, sir," said Peter, "I admire it."

"You must, then, give me your undivided attention," said Vilna Lutz. He picked up his wooden foot and beat it against the floor. "This is important. This is the work of your father I am speaking of. This is a man's work."

Peter looked down at the toy soldiers and thought about his father in a field full of mud, a bayonet wound in his side. He thought about his father bleeding. He thought about him dying.

And then he remembered the dream of Adele, the weight of her in his arms and the golden light that had been outside the door. He remembered his father holding him, catching him, in the garden.

And for the first time, soldiering did not, in any way, seem like a man's work to Peter. Instead it seemed like foolishness — a horrible, terrible, nightmarish foolishness.

"So," said Vilna Lutz. He cleared his throat. "As I was saying, as I was illuminating, as I was elucidating, yes, these men, these brave, brave soldiers, under the direct orders of the brilliant General Von Flickenhamenger, came around from behind. They outflanked the enemy. And that, ultimately, is how the battle was won. Does that make sense?"

Peter looked down at the soldiers arranged carefully and just so. He looked up at Vilna Lutz's face and then down again at the soldiers.

"No," he said at last.

"No?"

"No. It does not make sense."

"Well, then, tell me what you see when you look upon it, if you do not see the sense of it."

"I look upon it and wish that it could be undone."

"Undone?" said Vilna Lutz.

"Yes. Undone. No wars. No soldiers."

Vilna Lutz stared at Peter with his mouth agape and the point of his beard trembling.

Peter, looking back at him, felt something unbearably hot rise up in his throat; he knew that now the words would finally come.

"She lives," he said. "That is what the fortune-teller told me. She lives, and an elephant will lead me to her. And because an elephant has come out of nowhere, out of nothing, I believe her. Not you. I do not — I cannot — any longer believe you."

"What is this you are talking about? Who lives?"

"My sister," said Peter.

"Your sister? Am I mistaken? Were we speaking of the domestic sphere? No. We were not. We were speaking of battles, you and I. We were speaking of the brilliance of generals and the bravery of foot soldiers." Vilna Lutz beat his wooden foot against the floorboards. "Battles and bravery and strategy, that is what we were speaking of."

"Where is she? What happened to her?"

The old soldier grimaced. He put down the foot and pointed his index finger heavenwards. "I told you. I have told you many times. She is with your mama, in heaven."

"I heard her cry," said Peter. "I held her."

"Bah," said Vilna Lutz. His finger, still pointing heavenwards, trembled. "She did not cry. She could not cry. Stillborn. She was stillborn. The breath never reached her lungs. She never drew breath."

"She cried. I remember. I know it to be true."

"And what of it? What if she did cry? That she cried does not mean that she lived — not at all, not at all. If every babe who cried were still alive, well, then, the world would be a very crowded place indeed."

"Where is she?" said Peter.

Vilna Lutz let out a small sob.

"Where?" said Peter again.

"I do not know," said the old soldier. "The midwife took her away. She said that she was too small, that she could not possibly put something so delicate into the hands of one such as me."

"You said she died. Time and again, you told me that she was dead. You lied."

"Do not call it a lie. Call it scientific conjecture. Babes without their mothers often will not live. And she was so small."

"You lied to me."

"No, no, Private Duchene. I lied *for* you,

to protect you. What could you have done if you had known? It would only have hurt your heart to know. I cared for you — you, who would and could become a soldier like your father, a man I admired. I did not take your sister, because the midwife would not let me; she was so small, so impossibly small. What do I know of infants and their needs? I know of soldiering, not mothering."

Peter got up from the floor. He walked to the window and stood looking out at the cathedral spire, the birds wheeling in the air.

"I am done talking now, sir," said Peter. "Tomorrow I will go to the elephant and then I will find my sister and I will be done with you. I am done, too, with being a soldier, because soldiering is a useless and pointless thing."

"Do not say something so terrible," said Vilna Lutz. "Think of your father."

"I am thinking of my father," said Peter.

And he was.

He was thinking of his father in the garden.

And he was thinking of him on the battlefield, bleeding to death.

## Chapter Ten

The weather worsened.

Although it did not seem possible, it became colder.

Although it did not seem possible, it grew darker.

It would not snow.

And in the cold, dark dorm room at the Orphanage of the Sisters of Perpetual Light, Adele continued to dream of the elephant.

The dream was so persistent that Adele could, after a time, repeat verbatim the words that the elephant spoke to Sister Marie when she came to the door. There was, in particular, one sentence that the elephant spoke that was so full of beauty and promise that Adele took to saying it to herself during the day: "'It is the one you are calling Adele I am coming for to keep.'" She said these words over and over, as if they were a poem or a blessing or a prayer. "It is the one you are calling Adele I am coming for to keep; it is the one you are calling Adele I am coming for to keep—'"

"Who are you talking to?" said an older girl named Lisette.

She and Adele were in the orphanage kitchen together, bent over a bucket, peeling potatoes.

"No one," said Adele.

"But your lips were moving," said Lisette.

"I saw them move. You were saying something."

"I was saying the elephant's words," said Adele.

"The elephant's words?"

"The elephant from my dreams. She speaks to me."

"Oh, of course, silly me, the speaking elephant from your dreams," said Lisette. She snorted.

"The elephant knocks at the door and asks for me," said Adele. She lowered her voice. "I believe that she has come to take me away from here."

"To take you away?" said Lisette. Her eyes narrowed. "And where would she take you?"

"Home," said Adele.

"Ha! Listen to her!" said Lisette. "Home." She snorted again. "How old are you?"

"Six," said Adele. "Almost seven."

"Yes, well, you are very exceptionally,

amazingly stupid for almost seven years old,"
said Lisette.

There came a knock at the kitchen door.

"Hark!" said Lisette. "Someone knocks!
Maybe it is an elephant." She got up and went
to the door and threw it wide. "Look, Adele,"
she said, turning back with a terrible smile on
her face. "Look who is here. It is an elephant
come to take you home."

There was not, of course, an elephant at
the door. Instead, there stood the neighbour-
hood beggar and his dog.

"We have nothing to give you," said Lisette
in a loud voice. "We're orphans. This is an
orphanage." She stamped her foot.

"We have nothing to give," sang the beggar, "but look, Adele, an elephant, and this is
wonderful news."

Adele looked at the beggar's face and saw
that he was truly, terribly hungry.

"Look, Adele, an elephant," he sang,

"but you must know that the truth is always changing."

"Don't sing," said Lisette. She slammed the door shut and came and sat down next to Adele. "You see, now, who comes and knocks at the door here? Blind dogs. And beggars who sing meaningless songs. Do you think they have come to take us home?"

"He was hungry," said Adele. She felt an unsolicited tear roll down her cheek. It was followed by another and then another.

"So what?" said Lisette. "Who do you know who isn't hungry?"

"No one," answered Adele truthfully. She herself was always hungry.

"Yes," said Lisette, "we are all hungry. So what?"

Adele could think of nothing to say in reply.

All she had were the words of a dream elephant. They were not much, but they were hers, and she began again to say them to herself: "'It is the one you are calling Adele I am coming for to keep; it is the one you are calling Adele I am coming for to keep; it is the one you are calling Adele—'"

"Quit moving your lips," said Lisette. "Can't you see that no one intends to come for us?"

## Chapter Eleven

On the first Saturday of the month, the city of Baltese turned out to see the elephant. The line snaked from the home of the Countess Quintet out into the street and down the hill as far as the eye could see. There were young men with waxed moustaches and pomaded hair, and old ladies dressed in borrowed finery, their wrinkled faces scrubbed clean. There were candle makers who smelled of

warm beeswax, washerwomen with rough-
ened hands and hopeful faces, babies still
at their mothers' breasts, and old men who
leaned heavily on canes.

Milliners stood with their heads held
high, their latest creations displayed proudly
on their heads. Lamplighters, their eyes
heavy from lack of sleep, stood next to street
sweepers, who held their brooms before them
as if they were swords. Priests and fortune-
tellers stood side by side and eyed each other
with distaste and wariness.

Everyone, it seemed, was there: the
whole city of Baltese stood in line to see
the elephant.

And everyone, each person, had hopes and
dreams, wishes for revenge, and desires for
love.

They stood together.

They waited.

And secretly, deep within their hearts,

even though they knew it could not truly be so, they each expected that the mere sight of the elephant would somehow deliver them, would make their wishes and hopes and desires come true.

Peter stood in line directly behind a man who was dressed entirely in black and who had atop his head a black hat with an exceptionally wide brim. The man rocked from heel to toe, muttering, "The dimensions of an elephant are most impressive. The dimensions of an elephant are impressive in the extreme. I will now detail for you the dimensions of an elephant."

Peter listened carefully, because he would have liked very much to know the actual dimensions of an elephant. It seemed like good information to have; but the man in the black hat never arrived at the point of announcing the figures. Instead, after insisting that

he would detail the dimensions, he paused dramatically, took a deep breath and then began again, rocking from heel to toe and saying, "The dimensions of an elephant are most impressive. The dimensions of an elephant are impressive in the extreme..."

The line inched slowly forward, and mercifully, late in the afternoon, the black-hatted man's mutterings were eclipsed by the music of a beggar who stood singing, his hand outstretched, a black dog at his side.

The beggar's voice was sweet and gentle and full of hope. Peter closed his eyes and listened. The song placed a steady hand on his heart. It comforted him.

"Look, Adele," sang the beggar. "Here is your elephant."

*Adele.*

Peter turned his head and looked directly at the beggar, and the man, incredibly, sang her name again.

*Adele.*

"Let him hold her," his mother had said to the midwife the night that the baby was born, the night that his mother died.

"I do not think I should," said the midwife. "He is too young himself."

"No, let him hold her," his mother said.

And so the midwife gave him the crying baby. And he held her.

"This is what you must remember," said his mother. "She is your sister, and her name is Adele. She belongs to you, and you belong to her. That is what you must remember. Can you do that?"

Peter nodded.

"You will take care of her?"

Peter nodded again.

"Can you promise me, Peter?"

"Yes," he said, and then he said that terrible, wonderful word once more, in case his mother had not heard him. "Yes."

And Adele, as if she had heard and understood him too, stopped crying.

Peter opened his eyes. The beggar was gone, and from ahead of him in line came the now achingly familiar words: "The dimensions of an elephant..."

Peter took off his hat and put it back on again and then took it off, working hard at keeping the tears inside.

He had promised.

He had *promised*.

He received a shove from behind.

"Are you juggling your hat, or are you waiting in line?" said a gruff voice.

"Waiting in line," said Peter.

"Well, then, move forward, why don't you?"

Peter put his hat on his head and stepped forward smartly, like the soldier, the very good soldier, he had once trained to become.

\* \* \*

In the home of the Count and Countess Quintet, inside the ballroom, as the people filed by her, touching her, pulling at her, leaning against her, spitting, laughing, weeping, praying and singing, the elephant stood broken-hearted.

There were too many things that she did not understand.

Where were her brothers and sisters? Her mother?

Where were the long grass and the bright sun? Where were the hot days and the dark pools of shade and the cool nights?

The world had become too cold and confusing and chaotic to bear.

She stopped reminding herself of her name.

She decided that she would like to die.

## Chapter Twelve

The Countess Quintet had discovered that it was a somewhat messy affair to have an elephant in one's ballroom, and so, for matters of delicacy and cleanliness, she engaged the services of a small, extremely unobtrusive man whose job it was to stand behind the elephant, ever at the ready with a bucket and a shovel. The little man's back was bent and twisted, and because of this, it was almost impossible

for him to lift his face and look directly at anyone or anything.

He viewed everything sideways.

His name was Bartok Whynn, and before
he came to stand perpetually and forever at
the rear of the elephant, he had been a stonecutter who laboured high atop the city's largest
and most magnificent cathedral, working at
coaxing gargoyles from stone. Bartok Whynn's
gargoyles were well and truly frightening,
each different from the others and each more
horrifying than the one that had preceded it.

On a day in late summer, the summer
before the winter the elephant arrived in
Baltese, Bartok Whynn was engaged in the
task of bringing to life the most gruesome
gargoyle he had yet conceived, when he lost
his footing and fell. Because he was so high
atop the cathedral, it took him quite a long
time to reach the ground. The stonecutter had
time to think.

What he thought was, I am going to die.

This thought was followed by another thought: But I know something. I know something. What is it I know?

It came to him then. Ah, yes, I know what I know. Life is funny. That is what I know.

And falling through the air, he actually laughed aloud. The people on the street below heard him. They exclaimed over it among themselves. "Imagine a man falling to his death and laughing all the while!"

Bartok Whynn hit the ground, and his broken, bleeding and unconscious body was borne by his fellow stonecutters through the streets and home to his wife, who equivocated between sending for the funeral director and sending for the doctor.

She settled, finally, upon the doctor.

"His back is broken and he cannot survive," the doctor told Bartok Whynn's wife. "It is not possible for any man to survive such a fall. That he has lived this long is some miracle that we cannot understand and should only be grateful for. Surely it has some meaning beyond our understanding."

Bartok Whynn, who had, up to this point, been unconscious, made a small sound and took hold of the doctor's greatcoat and gestured for him to come close.

"Wait a moment," said the doctor. "Attend, madam. Now he will deliver the words, the important words, the great message that he has been spared in order to speak. You may give those words to me, sir. Give them to me." And with a flourish, the doctor flung his coat to the side and bent over Bartok's broken body and offered him his ear.

"Heeeeeeeeeee," whispered Bartok Whynn into the doctor's ear, "heee heee."

"What does he say?" said the wife.

The doctor stood up. His face was very

pale. "Your husband says nothing," he said.

"Nothing?" said the wife.

Bartok tugged again at the doctor's coat. Again the doctor bent and offered his ear, but this time with markedly less enthusiasm.

"Heeeeeeeeeeee," laughed Bartok Whynn into the doctor's ear, "heeeee heee."

The doctor stood up. He straightened his coat.

"He said nothing?" said the wife. She wrung her hands.

"Madam," said the doctor, "he laughs. He has lost his mind. His life is to follow. I tell you he will not — he cannot — live."

But the stonecutter's broken back healed in its strange and crooked way, and he lived.

Before the fall Bartok Whynn was a dour man who measured five feet nine inches and who laughed, at most, once a fortnight. After the fall he measured four feet eleven inches and he laughed darkly, knowingly, daily, hourly, at everything and nothing at all. The whole of existence struck him as cause for hilarity.

He went back to work high atop the cathedral. He held the chisel in his hand. He stood before the stone. But he could not stop laughing long enough to coax anything from it. He laughed and laughed, his hands shook, the stone remain untouched, the gargoyles did not appear, and Bartok Whynn was dismissed from his job.

That is how he came, in the end, to stand behind the elephant with a bucket and a shovel. His new position in life did not at all, in any way, diminish his propensity for hilarity. If anything, if possible, he laughed more. He laughed harder.

Bartok Whynn laughed.

And so when Peter, late in the day, in the perpetual, unvarying gloom of the Baltesian winter afternoon, finally stepped through the elephant door and into the brightly lit ballroom of the Countess Quintet, what he heard was laughter.

The elephant, at first, was not visible to him.

There were so many people gathered around her that she was obscured entirely. But then, as Peter got closer and closer still, she was finally, and at last, revealed. She was both larger and smaller than he had expected her to be. And the sight of her, her head hung low, her eyes closed, made his heart feel tight in his chest.

"Move along — ha ha hee!" shouted a small man with a shovel. "Wheeeeee! You must move along so that everyone, *everyone*, may view the elephant."

Peter took his hat from his head. He held it over his heart. He inched close enough to put his hand on the rough, solid flank of the elephant. She was moving, swaying from side to side. The warmth of her astonished him. Peter shoved at the people surrounding him and managed to get his face up next to hers so that he could say what he had come to say, ask what he had come to ask.

"Please," he said, "you know where my sister is. Can you tell me?"

And then he felt terrible for saying anything at all. She seemed so tired and sad. Was she asleep?

"Move along, move along — ha ha hee!" shouted the little man.

"Please," whispered Peter to the elephant, "could you ... I need you to ... could you ... would it be possible for you to open your eyes? Could you look at me?"

The elephant stopped swaying. She held very still. And then, after a long moment, she

opened her eyes and looked directly at him. She delivered to him a single, great, despairing glance.

And Peter forgot about Adele and his mother and the fortune-teller and the old soldier and his father and battlefields and lies and promises and predictions. He forgot about everything except for the terrible truth of what he saw, what he understood in the elephant's eyes.

She was heartbroken.

She had to go home.

The elephant had to go home or she would surely die.

As for the elephant, when she opened her eyes and saw the boy, she felt a small shock go through her.

He was looking at her as if he knew her.

He was looking at her as if he understood.

For the first time since she had come

through the roof of the opera house, the elephant felt something akin to hope.

"Don't worry," Peter whispered to her. "I will make sure that you get home."

She stared at him.

"I promise," said Peter.

"Next!" shouted the little man with the shovel. "You must, you simply *must*, move along. Ha ha hee! There are others waiting to see the — ha ha hee! — elephant too."

Peter stepped away.

He turned. He walked without looking back, out of the ballroom of the Countess Quintet, through the elephant door, and into the dark world.

He had made a promise to the elephant, but what kind of promise was it?

It was the worst kind of promise; it was yet another promise that he could not keep.

How could he, Peter, make sure that an

elephant got home? He did not even know where the elephant's home was. Was it Africa? India? Where were those places, and how could he get an elephant there?

He might just as well have promised the elephant that he would secure for her an enormous set of wings.

It is horrible, what I have done, thought Peter. It is terrible. I should never have promised. Nor should I have asked the fortune-teller my question. I should not have, no. I should have left things as they were. And what the magician did was a terrible thing too. He should never have brought the elephant here. I am glad that he is in prison. They should never, ever let him out. He is a terrible man to do such a thing.

And then Peter was struck by a thought so wondrous that he stopped walking. He put his hat on his head. He took it off. He put it back on again. He took it off.

*The magician.*

If the world held magic powerful enough to make the elephant appear, then there had to exist, too, magic in equal measure, magic powerful enough to undo what had been done.

There had to be magic that could send the elephant home.

"The magician," said Peter out loud, and then he said, "Leo Matienne!"

He put his hat on his head. He began to run.

## Chapter Thirteen

Leo Matienne opened the door of his apartment. He was barefoot. A napkin was tied around his neck, and a bit of carrot and a crumb of bread were caught in his moustache. The smell of mutton stew wafted out into the cold, dark street.

"It is Peter Augustus Duchene!" said Leo Matienne. "And he has his hat on his head. And he is here, on the ground, instead of up there, acting like a cuckoo in a clock."

"I am very sorry to disturb you at your dinner," said Peter, "but I must see the magician."

"You must do what?"

"I need you to take me to the prison so that I may see the magician. You are a policeman, an officer of the law; surely they will let you inside."

"Who is it?" called Gloria Matienne. She came to the door and stood beside her husband.

"Good evening, Madam Matienne," said Peter. He took off his hat and bowed to Gloria.

"And a good evening to you," said Gloria.

"Yes, good evening," said Peter. He put his hat back on his head. "I am sorry to disturb you at your dinner, but I need to go to the prison immediately."

"He needs to go to the prison?" said Gloria Matienne to her husband. "Is that what he said? Have mercy! What kind of request is that for a child to make? And look at him, please. He is so skinny that you can see right through him. He is ... what is the word?"

"Transparent?" said Leo.

"Yes," said Gloria, "exactly that. Transparent. Does that old man not feed you? In addition to no love, is there no food in that attic room?"

"There is bread," said Peter. "And also fish, but they are very small fish, exceedingly small."

"You must come inside," said Gloria. "That is the thing which you must immediately do. You must come inside."

"But—" said Peter.

"Come inside," said Leo. "We will talk."

"Come inside," said Gloria Matienne. "First we will eat, and *then* we will talk."

There was, in the apartment of Leo and Gloria Matienne, a wonderful fire blazing, and the kitchen table was pulled up close to the hearth.

"Sit," said Leo.

Peter sat. His legs were shaking and his heart was beating fast, as if he were still running. "I do not think that there is much time," he said. "I do not think that there is enough time, truly, to dine."

Gloria put a bowl of stew in Peter's hands. "Eat," she said.

Peter raised the spoon to his lips. He chewed. He swallowed.

It had been a long time since he had eaten anything besides tiny fish and old bread.

And so when Peter had his first bite of stew, it overwhelmed him. The warmth of it, the richness of it, knocked him backwards; it was as if a gentle hand had pushed him when he was not expecting it. Everything he had lost came flooding back: the garden, his father, his mother, his sister, the promises that he had made and could not keep.

"What's this?" said Gloria Matienne. "The boy is crying."

"Shh," said Leo. He put his hand on Peter's shoulder. "Shh. Don't worry, Peter. Everything will be good. All will be well. We will do together whatever it is that needs to be done. But for now, you must eat."

Peter nodded. He raised his spoon. Again he chewed and swallowed, and again he was overcome. He could not help it. He could not stop the tears; they flowed down his cheeks and into the bowl. "It is very good stew, Madam Matienne," he managed to say. "Truly, it is excellent stew."

His hands shook; the spoon rattled against the bowl.

"Here, now," said Gloria Matienne, "don't spill it."

It is gone, thought Peter. All of it is gone! And there is no way to get it back.

"Eat," said Leo Matienne again, very gently.

Peter looked the truth of what he had lost full in the face.

And then he ate.

When Peter was done, Leo Matienne sat down in the chair beside him and said, "Now you must tell us everything."

"Everything?" said Peter.

"Yes, everything," said Leo Matienne. He leaned back in his chair. "Begin at the beginning."

Peter started in the garden. He began his story with his father throwing him up high in the air and catching him. He began with his mother dressed all in white, laughing, her stomach round like a balloon.

"The sky was purple," said Peter. "The lamps were lit."

"Yes," said Leo Matienne. "I can see it all very well. And where is your father now?"

"He was a soldier," said Peter, "and he died on the battlefield. Vilna Lutz served with him and fought beside him. He was his friend. He came to our house to deliver the news of my father's death."

"Vilna Lutz," said Gloria Matienne, and it was as if she were uttering a curse.

"When my mother heard the news, the baby started to come: my sister, Adele." Peter stopped. He took a deep breath. "My sister was born, and my mother died. Before she died, I promised her that I would always watch out for the baby. But then I could not, because the midwife took the baby away and Vilna Lutz took me with him, to teach me how to be a soldier."

Gloria Matienne stood. "Vilna Lutz!" she shouted. She shook a fist at the ceiling. "I will have a word with him."

"Sit, please," said Leo Matienne.

Gloria sat.

"And what became of your sister?" said Leo to Peter.

"Vilna Lutz told me that she died. He said that she was born dead, stillborn."

Gloria Matienne gasped.

"He said that. But he lied. He lied. He has admitted that he lied. She is not dead."

"Vilna Lutz!" said Gloria Matienne. Again she leaped to her feet and shook her fist at the ceiling.

"First the fortune-teller told me that she lives, and then my own dream told me the same. And the fortune-teller told me also that the elephant — *an* elephant — would lead me to her. But today, this afternoon, I saw the elephant, Leo Matienne, and I know that she will die if she cannot go home. She must go home. The magician must return her there."

Leo crossed his arms and tipped his chair back on two legs.

"Don't do that," said Gloria. She sat down again. "It is very bad for the chair."

Leo Matienne came slowly forward until all four chair legs were again resting on the floor. He smiled. "What if?" he said.

"Oh, don't start," said his wife. "Please, don't start."

"Why not?"

From somewhere high above them, there came a muffled *thump*, the sound of Vilna Lutz beating his wooden foot on the floor, demanding something.

"Could it be?" said Leo.

"Yes," said Peter. He did not look up at the ceiling. He kept his eyes on Leo Matienne. "What if?" he said to the policeman.

"Why not?" said Leo back to him. He smiled.

"Enough," said Gloria.

"No," said Leo Matienne, "not enough. Never enough. We must ask ourselves these questions as often as we dare. How will the world change if we do not question it?"

"The world cannot be changed," said Gloria. "The world is what the world is and has for ever been."

"No," said Leo Matienne softly, "I will not believe that. For here is Peter standing before us, asking us to make it something different."

*Thump, thump, thump,* went Vilna Lutz's foot above them.

Gloria looked up at the ceiling. She looked over at Peter.

She shook her head. She nodded her head. And then, slowly, she nodded it again.

"Yes," said Leo Matienne, "yes, that is what I thought too." He stood and took the napkin from his neck. "It is time for us to go to the prison."

He put his arms around his wife and pulled

her close. She rested her cheek against his for a moment, and then she pulled away from Leo and turned to Peter.

"You," she said.

"Yes," said Peter. He stood straight before her, like a soldier awaiting inspection, and so he was not prepared at all when she grabbed him and pulled him close, enveloping him in the smell of mutton stew and starch and green grass.

Oh, to be held!

He had forgotten entirely what it meant. He wrapped his arms around Gloria Matienne and began, again, to cry.

"There," she said. She rocked him back and forth. "There, you foolish, beautiful boy who wants to change the world. There, there. And who could keep from loving you? Who could keep from loving a boy so brave and true?"

## Chapter Fourteen

In the house of the countess, in the dark and empty ballroom, the elephant slept. She dreamed she was walking across a wide savannah. The sky above her was a brilliant blue. She could feel the warmth of the sun on her back. In her dream the boy appeared a long way ahead of her and stood waiting.

When she at last drew close to him, he looked at her as he had done that afternoon.

But he said nothing. He simply fell into step beside her.

They walked together through the tall grass, and the elephant, in her dream, thought that this was a wonderful thing, to walk beside the boy. She felt that things were exactly as they should be, and she was happy.

The sun was so warm!

In the prison the magician lay upon his cloak, staring up at the window, hoping for the clouds to break and the bright star to appear.

He could no longer sleep.

Every time he closed his eyes, he saw the elephant crashing through the ceiling of the opera house and landing on top of Madam LaVaughn. The image bedevilled him to the point where he could get no rest, no respite. All he could think of was the elephant and the amazing, stupendous magic he had performed to call her forth.

At the same time, he was achingly, devastatingly lonely, and he wished, with the whole of his heart, to see a face, any human face. He would have been delighted, pleased beyond measure, to gaze upon even the accusatory, pleading countenance of the crippled Madam LaVaughn. If she appeared beside him right now, he would show her the star that was sometimes visible through his window. He would say to her, "Have you, in truth, ever seen something so heartbreakingly lovely? What are we to make of a world where stars shine bright in the midst of so much darkness and gloom?"

All of which is to say that the magician was awake that night when the outer door of the prison clanged open and two sets of footsteps sounded down the long corridor.

He stood.

He put on his cloak.

He looked out through the bars of his cell

and saw the light of a lantern shining in the darkened corridor. His heart leaped inside him. He called out to the approaching light.

And what did the magician say?

You know full well the words he spoke.

"I intended only lilies!" shouted the magician. "Please, I intended only a bouquet of lilies."

In the light from the lantern that Leo Matienne held aloft, Peter could see the magician all too clearly. His beard was long and wild, his fingernails ragged and torn, his cloak covered in a patina of mould. His eyes burned bright, but they were the eyes of a cornered animal: desperate and pleading and angry all at once.

Peter's heart sank. This man did not look as if he could perform any magic at all, much less the huge magic, the tremendous magic, of sending an elephant home.

"Who are you?" said the magician. "Who has sent you?"

"My name is Leo Matienne," said Leo, "and this is Peter Augustus Duchene, and we have come to speak to you about the elephant."

"Of course, of course," said the magician. "What else would you speak to me of but the elephant?"

"We want you to do the magic that will send her home," said Peter.

The magician laughed; it was not a pleasant sound. "Send her home, you say? And why would I do that?"

"Because she will die if you do not," said Peter.

"And why will she die?"

"She is homesick," said Peter. "I think that her heart is broken."

"A homesick, broken-hearted magic trick," said the magician. He laughed again. He shook his head. "It was all so magnificent when it happened; it was all so wondrous when it occurred — you would not believe it; truly you would not. And look what it has come to."

Somewhere in the prison, someone was crying. It was the kind of strangled weeping that Vilna Lutz sometimes gave himself over to when he thought that Peter was asleep.

The world is broken, thought Peter, and it cannot be fixed.

The magician kept still, his head pressed against the bars. The sound of the prisoner weeping rose and fell, rose and fell. And then Peter saw that the magician was crying too; great, lonely tears rolled down his face and disappeared into his beard.

Maybe it was not too late after all.

"I believe," said Peter very quietly.

"What do you believe?" said the magician without moving.

"I believe that things can still be set right.

I believe that you can perform the necessary magic."

The magician shook his head. "No." He said the word quietly, as if he were speaking it to himself. "No."

There was a long silence.

Leo Matienne cleared his throat, once, and then again. He opened his mouth and spoke two simple words. He said, "What if?"

The magician raised his head then and looked at the policeman. "What if?" he said. "'What if?' is a question that belongs to magic."

"Yes," said Leo, "to magic and also to the world in which we live every day. So: what if? What if you merely tried?"

"I tried already," said the magician. "I tried and failed to send her back." The tears continued to roll down his face. "You must understand: I did not want to send her back; she was the finest magic I have ever performed."

"To return her to where she belongs would be a fine magic too," said Leo Matienne.

"So you say," said the magician. He looked at Leo Matienne and then at Peter and then back again at Leo Matienne.

"Please," said Peter.

The light from the lantern in Leo's outstretched arm flickered, and the magician's shadow, cast on the wall behind him, reared back suddenly and then grew larger. The shadow stood apart from him as if it were another creature entirely, watching over him, waiting anxiously, along with Peter, for the magician to decide what seemed to be the fate of the entire universe.

"Very well," said the magician at last. "I will try. But I will need two things. I will need the elephant, for I cannot make her disappear without her being present. And I will need Madam LaVaughn. You must bring both the elephant and the noblewoman here to me."

"But that is impossible," said Peter.

"Magic is always impossible," said the magician. "It begins with the impossible and ends with the impossible and is impossible in between. That is why it is magic."

## Chapter Fifteen

Madam LaVaughn was often kept awake at night by shooting pains in her legs. And because she was awake, she insisted that the whole household stay awake with her.

Further, she insisted that they listen again to the story of how she had dressed for the theatre that night, how she had walked into the building (Walked! On her own two legs!) entirely and absolutely innocent of the fate that awaited her inside. She insisted that the gardener and the cook, the serving maids and the chambermaids, pretend to be interested as she spoke again of how the magician had selected her from among the sea of hopefuls.

"'Who, then, will come before me and receive my magic?' Those were his exact words," said Madam LaVaughn.

The assembled servants listened (or pretended to) as the noblewoman spoke of the elephant falling from nowhere, of how one minute the notion of an elephant was inconceivable and the next the elephant was an irrefutable fact in her lap.

"Crippled," said Madam LaVaughn in conclusion, "crippled by an elephant that came through the roof!"

The servants knew these last words so well, so intimately, that they mouthed them along with her, whispering the phrases together as if they were participating in some odd and arcane religious ceremony.

This, then, is what was taking place in the house of Madam LaVaughn that evening when there came a knock at the door, and the butler appeared beside Hans Ickman to announce that there was a policeman waiting outside and that this policeman absolutely insisted on speaking to Madam LaVaughn.

"At this hour?" said Hans Ickman.

But he followed the butler to the door, and there, indeed, stood a policeman, a short man with a ridiculously large moustache.

The policeman stepped forward and bowed and said, "Good evening. I am Leo Matienne. I serve with Her Majesty's police force. I am not, however, here on official business. I have come instead with a most unusual personal request for Madam LaVaughn."

"Madam LaVaughn cannot be disturbed," said Hans Ickman. "The hour is late, and she is in pain."

"Please," said a small voice.

Hans Ickman saw then that there was a boy standing behind the policeman and that he held a soldier's hat in his hand.

"It is important," said the boy.

The manservant looked into the boy's eyes and saw himself, young again and still capable of believing in miracles, standing on the bank of the river with his brothers, the white dog suspended in mid-air.

"Please," said the boy.

And suddenly it came to Hans Ickman, the name of the little white dog. Rose. She was called Rose. And remembering was like fitting a piece of a puzzle into place. He felt a wonderful certainty. The impossible, he thought, the impossible is about to happen again.

He looked past the policeman and the boy and into the darkness beyond them. He saw something swirl through the air. A snowflake. And then another. And another.

"Come in," said Hans Ickman. He swung the door wide. "You must come inside now. The snow has begun."

It had indeed begun to snow. It was snowing over the whole of the city of Baltese.

The snow fell in the darkened alleys and on the newly repaired tiles of the opera house. It settled atop the turrets of the prison and on the roof of the Apartments Polonaise. At the home of the Countess Quintet the snow worked to outline the graceful curve of the handle on the elephant door; and at the cathedral it formed fanciful and slightly ridiculous caps for the heads of the gargoyles, who crouched together, gazing down at the city in disgust and envy.

The snow danced around the circles of light that pulsed from the lamps lining the wide boulevards of the city of Baltese. The

snow fell in a curtain of white all around the bleak and unprepossessing building that was the Orphanage of the Sisters of Perpetual Light, as if it were working very hard to hide the place from view.

The snow, at last, fell.

And as it snowed, Bartok Whynn dreamed.

He dreamed of carving. He dreamed of doing the work he knew and loved: coaxing figures from stone. Only, in his dream, he did not carve gargoyles, but humans. One was a boy wearing a hat; another, a man with a moustache; and another, a woman sitting, with a man standing to attention behind her.

And each time a new person appeared beneath his hand, Bartok Whynn was astonished and deeply moved.

"You," he said as he worked, "and you and you. And you."

He smiled.

And because it was a dream, the people he had fashioned from stone smiled back at him.

As the snow fell, Sister Marie, who sat by the door at the Orphanage of the Sisters of Perpetual Light, dreamed too.

She dreamed that she was flying high over the world, her habit spread out on either side of her like dark wings.

She was terribly pleased, because she had always, secretly, deep within her heart, believed that she could fly. And now here she was, doing what she had long suspected she could do, and she could not deny that it was gratifying in the extreme.

Sister Marie looked down at the world below her and saw millions and millions of stars and thought, I am not flying over the earth at all. Why, I am flying higher than that. I am flying over the very tops of the stars. I am looking down at the sky.

And then she realized that no, no, it *was* the earth that she was flying over, and that she was looking not at the stars but at the creatures of the world, and that they were all, they were each — beggars, dogs, orphans, kings, elephants, soldiers — emitting pulses of light.

The whole of creation glowed.

Sister Marie's heart grew large in her chest, and her heart, expanding in such a way, allowed her to fly higher and then higher still — but no matter how high she flew, she never lost sight of the glowing earth below her.

"Oh," said Sister Marie out loud in her sleep, in her chair by the door, "how wonderful. Didn't I know it? I did. I did. I knew it all along."

## Chapter Sixteen

Hans Ickman pushed Madam LaVaughn's wheelchair, and Leo Matienne had hold of Peter's hand. The four of them moved quickly through the snowy streets. They were heading to the home of the countess.

"I do not understand," said Madam LaVaughn. "I find this all highly irregular."

"I believe the time has come," said Hans Ickman.

"The time? The time? The time for what?" said Madam LaVaughn. "Do not speak to me in riddles."

"The time for you to return to the prison."

"But it is the middle of the night, and the prison is that way," said Madam LaVaughn, flinging a heavily bejewelled hand behind her. "The prison is in entirely the opposite direction."

"There is something else that we must tend to first," said Leo Matienne.

"And what is that?" said Madam LaVaughn.

"We must retrieve the elephant from the home of the countess," said Peter, "and take her to the magician."

"Retrieve the elephant?" said Madam LaVaughn. "Retrieve the elephant? Take the elephant to the magician? Is he mad? Is the boy mad? Is the policeman mad? Has everyone gone mad?"

"Yes," said Hans Ickman after a long

moment. "I believe that is the case. Everyone has gone a little mad."

"Oh," said Madam LaVaughn, "very well. I see."

They were silent together then: the noblewoman and her servant, the policeman and the boy walking beside him. There was only the sound of the wheelchair moving through the snow and three pairs of footsteps striking the muffled cobblestones.

It was Madam LaVaughn who at last broke the silence. "Highly irregular," she said, "but quite interesting, very interesting indeed. Why, it seems as if anything could happen, anything at all."

"Exactly," said Hans Ickman.

In the prison, in his small cell, the magician paced back and forth. "And if they succeed?" he said. "If they manage, somehow, to bring the elephant here? Then there is no helping it.

I must speak the words. I must try to cast the spell again. I must work to send her back."

The magician paused in his pacing and looked up and out of his window and was amazed to see snowflake after snowflake dancing through the air.

"Oh, look," he said, even though he was alone. "It is snowing — how beautiful."

The magician stood very still. He stared at the falling snow.

And suddenly he did not care at all that he would have to undo the greatest thing he had ever done.

He had been so lonely, so desperately, hopelessly lonely for so long. He might very well spend the rest of his life in prison, alone. And he understood that what he wanted now was something much simpler, much more complicated than the magic he had performed. What he wanted was to turn to somebody and take hold of their hand and look up with them and marvel at the snow falling from the sky.

"This," he wanted to say to someone he loved and who loved him in return. "This."

Peter and Leo Matienne and Hans Ickman and Madam LaVaughn stood outside the home of the Countess Quintet; they stared together at the massive, imposing elephant door.

"Oh," said Peter.

"We will knock," said Leo Matienne. "That is where we will begin, with knocking."

"Yes," said Hans Ickman. "We will knock."

The three of them stepped forward and began to pound on the door.

Time stopped.

Peter had a terrible feeling that the whole of his life had been nothing but standing and knocking, asking to be let into some place that he was not even certain existed.

His fingers were cold. His knuckles hurt. The snow fell harder and faster.

"Perhaps this is a dream," said Madam LaVaughn from her chair. "Perhaps the whole thing has been nothing but a dream."

Peter remembered the door in the wheat field. He remembered holding Adele. And then he remembered the terrible, heartbroken look in the elephant's eyes.

"Please!" he shouted. "Please, you must let us in."

"Please!" shouted Leo Matienne.

"Yes," said Hans Ickman, "please."

And from the other side of the door came the screech of a deadbolt being thrown. And then another and another. And slowly, as if it were reluctant to do so, the door began to open. A small, bent man appeared. He stepped outside and looked up at the falling snow and laughed.

"Yes," he said. "You knocked?"

And then he laughed again.

\* \* \*

Bartok Whynn laughed even harder when Peter told him why they had come.

"You want — ha ha hee — to take the elephant from here to the — ha ha hee wheeeeee — to the magician in prison so that the magician may perform the magic to send the elephant — wheeeeee — home?"

He laughed so hard that he lost his balance and had to sit down in the snow.

"Whatever is so funny?" said Madam LaVaughn. "You must tell us so that we may laugh along with you."

"You may laugh along with me," said Bartok Whynn, "only if you find it funny to — ha ha hee — think of me dead. Imagine if the countess were to wake tomorrow and find that her elephant had disappeared, and that I, Bartok Whynn, was the one — ha ha hee — who had allowed the beast to be spirited away?"

The little man was shaken by a hilarity

so profound that his laughter disappeared altogether, and no sound at all came from his open mouth.

"But what if you were not here either?" said Leo Matienne. "What if you too were gone on the morrow?"

"What is that?" said Bartok Whynn. "What did you — ha ha hee — say?"

"I said," said Leo Matienne, "what if you, like the elephant, were gone to the place you were meant, after all, to be?"

Bartok Whynn stared up at Leo Matienne and Hans Ickman and Peter and Madam LaVaughn. They were all holding very still, waiting. He held still, too, and considered them, gathered together there in the falling snow.

And in the silence he at last recognized them.

They were the figures from his dream.

\* \* \*

In the ballroom of the Countess Quintet, when the elephant opened her eyes and saw the boy standing before her, she was not at all surprised.

She thought simply, You. Yes, you. I knew that you would come for me.

## Chapter Seventeen

It was the snow that woke the dog. He lifted his head. He sniffed.

Snow, yes. But there was another smell, the scent of something wild and large.

Iddo got to his feet. He stood to attention, his tail quivering.

He barked. And then he barked again, louder.

"Shh," said Tomas.

But the dog would not be silenced.

Something incredible was approaching. He knew it, absolutely, to be true. Something wonderful was going to happen, and he would be the one to announce it. He barked and barked and barked.

He worked with the whole of his heart to deliver the message.

Iddo barked.

Upstairs, in the dorm room of the Orphanage of the Sisters of Perpetual Light, Adele heard the dog barking. She got out of bed and walked to the window and looked out and saw the snow dancing and twirling and spinning in the light of the street lamp.

"Snow," she said, "just like in the dream." She leaned her elbows on the windowsill and looked out at the whitening world.

And then, through the curtain of falling snow, Adele saw the elephant. She was walking down the street. She was following a boy. There was a policeman and a man pushing a woman in a wheelchair and a small man who was bent sideways. And the beggar was there with them, and so was the black dog.

"Oh," said Adele.

She did not doubt her eyes. She did not wonder if she was dreaming. She simply turned from the window and ran in her bare feet down the dark stairway and into the great room and from there into the hallway and past the sleeping Sister Marie. She threw wide the door to the orphanage.

"Here!" she shouted. "Here I am!"

The black dog came running towards her through the snow. He danced circles around her, barking, barking, barking.

It was as if he were saying, "Here you are at last. We have been waiting for you. And here, at last, you are."

"Yes," said Adele to the dog, "here I am."

\* \* \*

The draught from the open door woke Sister
Marie.

"The door is unlocked!" she shouted. "The
door is always and for ever unlocked. You must
simply knock."

When she was fully awake, Sister Marie
saw that the door was, in fact, wide open and
that beyond the door, in the darkness, snow
was falling. She got up from her chair and
went to pull the door closed and saw that there
was an elephant in the street.

"Preserve us," said Sister Marie.

And then she saw Adele standing in the
snow, in her nightgown and with no shoes on
her feet.

"Adele!" Sister Marie shouted. "Adele!"

But it was not Adele who turned to look at
her. It was a boy with a hat in his hands.

"Adele?" he said.

He spoke the name as if it were a question

and an answer both, and his face was alight with wonder.

The whole of him, in fact, shone like one of the bright stars from Sister Marie's dream.

He picked her up because it was snowing and it was cold and her feet were bare, and because he had promised their mother long ago that he would always take care of her.

"Adele," he said. "Adele."

"Who are you?" she said.

"I am your brother."

"My brother?"

"Yes."

She smiled at him, a sweet smile of disbelief that turned suddenly to belief and then to joy. "My brother," she said. "What is your name?"

"Peter."

"Peter," she said. And then again, "Peter. Peter. And you brought the elephant."

"Yes," said Peter. "I brought her. Or she brought me; but in any case, it is all the same and just as the fortune-teller said." He laughed and turned. "Leo Matienne," he shouted, "this is my sister!"

"I know," said Leo Matienne. "I can see."

"Who is it?" said Madam LaVaughn. "Who is she?"

"The boy's sister," said Hans Ickman.

"I don't understand," Madam LaVaughn said.

"It's the impossible," said Hans Ickman. "The impossible has happened again."

Sister Marie walked out through the open door of the Orphanage of the Sisters of Perpetual Light and into the snowy street. She stood next to Leo Matienne.

"It is, after all, a wonderful thing to dream of an elephant," she said to Leo, "and then to have the dream come true."

"Yes," said Leo Matienne, "yes, it must be."

Bartok Whynn, who stood beside the nun and the policeman, opened his mouth to laugh and then found that he could not. "I must—" he said. "I must—" But he did not finish the sentence.

The elephant, meanwhile, stood in the falling snow and waited.

It was Adele who remembered her and said to her brother, "Surely the elephant must be cold. Where is she going? Where are you taking her?"

"Home," said Peter. "We are taking her home."

## Chapter Eighteen

Peter walked in front of the elephant. He carried Adele. Next to Peter walked Leo Matienne. Behind the elephant was Madam LaVaughn in her wheelchair, pushed by Hans Ickman, who was, in turn, followed by Bartok Whynn, and behind him was the beggar, Tomas, with Iddo at his heels. At the very end was Sister Marie, who for the first time in fifty years was not at the door of the Orphanage of the Sisters of Perpetual Light.

Peter led them, and as he walked through the snowy streets, each lamp post, each doorway, each tree, each gate and each brick leaped out at him and spoke to him. All the things of the world were things of wonder that whispered to him the same message. Each object spoke the words of the fortune-teller and the hope of his heart that had turned out, after all, to be true. *She lives, she lives, she lives.*

And she did live! Her breath was warm on his cheek.

She weighed nothing.

Peter could have happily carried her in his arms for all eternity.

The cathedral clock tolled midnight. A few minutes after the last note, the magician heard the great outer door of the prison open and then close again. The sound of footsteps echoed down the corridor. The steps were accompanied by the jangle of keys.

"Who comes now?" shouted the magician. "Announce yourself!"

There was no answer, only footsteps and the light from the lantern. And then the policeman came into view. He stood in front of the magician's cell and held up the keys and said, "They await you outside."

"Who?" said the magician. "Who awaits me?" His heart thumped in disbelief.

"Everyone," said Leo Matienne.

"You have succeeded? You have brought the elephant here? And Madam LaVaughn as well?"

"Yes," said the policeman.

"Merciful," said the magician. "Oh, merciful. And now it must be undone. Now I must try to undo it."

"Yes, now it all rests upon you," said Leo. He inserted the key into the lock and turned it and pushed open the door to the magician's cell.

"Come," said Leo Matienne. "We are, all of us, waiting."

There is as much magic in making things disappear as there is in making them appear. More, perhaps. The undoing is almost always more difficult than the doing.

The magician knew this full well, and so when he stepped outside into the cold and snowy night, free for the first time in months, he felt no joy. Instead he was afraid. What if he tried and failed again?

And then he saw the elephant, the magnificence of her, the reality of her, standing there in the snow.

She was so improbable, so beautiful, so magical.

But no matter; it would have to be done. He would have to try.

"There," said Madam LaVaughn to Adele,

who was in the noblewoman's lap, wrapped up tight and warm, "there he is. That is the magician."

"He does not look like a bad man," said Adele. "He looks sad."

"Yes, well, I am crippled," said Madam LaVaughn, "and that, I assure you, goes somewhat beyond sadness."

"Madam," said the magician. He turned away from the elephant and bowed to Madam LaVaughn.

"Yes?" she said to him.

"I intended only lilies," said the magician.

"But perhaps you do not understand," said Madam LaVaughn.

"Please," said Hans Ickman, "please, I beg you! Speak from your hearts."

"I intended lilies," continued the magician, "but in the clutches of a desperate desire to do something extraordinary, I called down a greater magic and inadvertently caused you a profound harm. I will now try to undo what I have done."

"But will I walk again?" said Madam LaVaughn.

"I do not think so," said the magician. "But I beg you to forgive me. I hope that you will forgive me."

She looked at him.

"Truly, I did not intend to harm you," he said. "That was never my intention."

Madam LaVaughn sniffed. She looked away.

"Please," said Peter, "the elephant. It is so cold, and she needs to go home, where it is warm. Can you not do your magic now?"

"Very well," said the magician. He bowed again to Madam LaVaughn. He turned to the elephant. "You must, all of you, step away, step back. Step back."

Peter put his hand on the elephant. He let it rest there for a moment. "I'm sorry," he said to her. "And I thank you for what you did. Thank you and goodbye." And then he stepped away from her too.

The magician walked, circling the elephant and muttering to himself. He thought about the star on view from his prison cell. He thought about the snow falling at last, and how what he had wanted more than anything was to show it to someone. He thought about Madam LaVaughn's face looking up into his, questioning, hoping.

And then he began to speak the words of the spell. He said the words backwards, and he said the spell backwards too. He said it, all of it, under his breath, with the profound hope that it would well and truly work, and with the knowledge, too, that there was only so much, after all, that could be undone, even by magicians.

He spoke the words.

The snow stopped.

The sky became suddenly, miraculously clear, and for a moment the stars, too many of them to count, shone bright. The planet Venus sat among them, glowing solemnly.

It was Sister Marie who noticed. "Look there," she said. "Look up." She pointed at the sky. They all looked: Bartok Whynn, Tomas, Hans Ickman, Madam LaVaughn, Leo Matienne, Adele.

Even Iddo raised his head.

Only Peter kept his eyes on the elephant and the magician who was walking around and around her, muttering the backward words of a backward spell that would send her home.

And so Peter was the only one to see her leave. He was the only one to witness the greatest magic trick that the magician ever performed.

The elephant was there, and then she was not.

It was as simple as that.

As soon as she was gone, the clouds returned, the stars disappeared from view, and it began again to snow.

It is incredible that the elephant, who had arrived in the city of Baltese with so much noise, left it in such a profound silence. When she at last disappeared, there was no noise at all, only the *tic-tic-tic* of the falling snow.

Iddo put his nose up in the air and sniffed. He let out a low, questioning bark.

"Yes," Tomas said to him, "gone."

"Ah, well," said Leo Matienne.

Peter bent over and looked at the four circular footprints left in the snow. "She is truly gone," he said. "I hope she is home."

When he raised his head, Adele was looking at him, her eyes round and astonished.

He smiled at her. "Home," he said.

And she smiled back at him, that same smile: disbelief, then belief, and finally joy.

The magician sank to his knees and put his head in his shaking hands. "I am done with it then, all of it. And I am sorry. Truly, I am."

Leo Matienne took hold of the magician's arm and pulled him to his feet.

"Are you going to put him back in prison?" said Adele.

"I must," said Leo Matienne.

And then Madam LaVaughn spoke. "No, no. It is pointless, after all, is it not?"

"What?" said Hans Ickman. "What did you say?"

"I said that it is pointless to return him to prison. What has happened has happened. I release him. I will press no charges. I will sign any and all statements to that effect. Let him go. Let him go."

Leo Matienne let go of the magician's arm, and the magician turned to Madam LaVaughn and bowed. "Madam," he said.

"Sir," she said back.

They let him walk away.

They watched his black cloak retreating slowly into the swirling snow. They watched, together, until it disappeared entirely from view.

And when he was gone, Madam LaVaughn felt some great weight suddenly flap its wings and break free of her. She laughed aloud. She put her arms around Adele and hugged her tight.

"The child is cold," she said. "We must go inside."

"Yes," said Leo Matienne. "Let's go inside."

And that, after all, is how it ended.

Quietly.

In a world muffled by the gentle, forgiving hand of snow.

## Chapter Nineteen

Iddo slept in front of the fire when he came to visit.

And Tomas sang.

They did not ever, the two of them, stay for long.

But they visited often enough that Leo and Gloria and Peter and Adele learned to sing along with Tomas his strange and beautiful songs of elephants and truth and wonderful news.

Often, when they were singing, there came from the attic apartment a knocking sound.

It was usually Adele who went up the stairs to ask Vilna Lutz what it was he wanted. He could never answer her properly. He could only say that he was cold and that he would like the window to be closed; sometimes, when he was in the grip of a particularly high fever, he would allow Adele to sit beside him and hold his hand.

"We must outflank the enemy!" he would shout. "Where, oh where, is my foot?"

And then, in despair, he would say, "I cannot take her. Truly, I cannot. She is too small."

"Shh," said Adele. "There, there."

She would wait until the old soldier fell asleep, and then she would go back down the stairs to where Gloria and Leo and her brother were waiting for her.

And when she walked into the room, it

was always, for Peter, as if she had been gone a very long time. His heart leaped up high inside him, astonished and overjoyed anew at the sight of her, and he remembered again the door from his dream and the golden field of wheat. All that light, and here was Adele before him: warm and safe and loved.

It was, after all, as he had once promised his mother it would be.


The magician became a goatherd and married a woman who had no teeth. She loved him, and he loved her, and they lived with their goats in a hut at the foot of a steep hill. Sometimes, on summer evenings, they climbed the hill and stood together and stared up at the constellations in the night sky.

The magician showed his wife the star that he had gazed upon so often in prison, the star that, he felt, had kept him alive.

"It is that one," he said, pointing. "No, it is that one."

"It makes no never mind which it was, Frederick," his wife said gently. "All of them are beautiful."

And they were.

The magician never again performed an act of magic.

The elephant lived a very long time. And in spite of what they say about the memory of elephants, she recalled none of what had happened. She did not remember the opera house or the magician or the countess or Bartok Whynn. She did not remember the snow that had fallen so mysteriously from the sky. Perhaps it was too painful for her to remember. Or maybe the whole of it seemed to her like nothing more than a terrible dream that was best forgotten.

Sometimes, though, when she was walking through the tall grass or standing in the shade of the trees, Peter's face would flash in front of her, and she was struck with a peculiar feeling of having been well and truly seen, of having at last been found, saved.

And then the elephant was grateful, although she did not know to whom and could not think why.

And as the elephant forgot the city of Baltese and its inhabitants, so they too forgot her. Her disappearance caused a stir and then was forgotten. She became to them a strange and unbelievable notion that faded with time. Soon no one spoke of her miraculous appearance or her inexplicable disappearance; all of it seemed too impossible to have ever happened to begin with, to have ever been true.

## Chapter Twenty

But it did happen.

And some small evidence of these marvellous events remains.

High atop the city's most magnificent cathedral, hidden among the glowering and resentful gargoyles, there is a carving of an elephant being led by a boy. The boy is carrying a girl, and one of his hands is resting on the elephant, while behind the elephant there is a magician and a policeman, a nun and a noblewoman, a manservant, a beggar and a dog, and finally, behind them all, at the end, a small bent man.

Each person has hold of another, each one is connected to the one before him, and all are looking forward, their heads held at such an angle that it seems as if they are looking into a bright light.

If you yourself ever journey to the city of Baltese, and if, once you are there, you question enough people, you will — I know; I do believe — find someone who can lead you, someone able to show you the way to that cathedral, to that truth that Bartok Whynn left carved there, high up in the stone.

*Acknowledgements*

These people walked with me
through a long winter's night:
Tracey Bailey, Karla Rydrych,
Lisa Beck, Jane St Anthony,
Cindy Rogers, Jane O'Reilly,
Jennifer Brown, Amy Schwantes,
Emily van Beek and Holly McGhee.
I am for ever in their debt.

www.themagicianselephant.com

# Coming
# April 2016

Turn the page to read an extract...

# Eight

"They seem like criminals to me," said Beverly. "That girl and her almost-invisible granny. They remind me of Bonnie and Clyde."

Raymie nodded, even though Louisiana and her grandmother did not remind her of anyone else she had ever seen or heard of.

"Do you even know who Bonnie and Clyde were?" asked Beverly.

"Bank robbers?" said Raymie.

"That's right," said Beverly. "Criminals. Those two look like they could rob a bank. And what kind of name is Louisiana, anyway? Louisiana is the name of a state. It's not what you call a person. That girl is probably operating under an assumed name. She's probably running from the law. That's why she seems so afraid in that rabbity kind of way. I tell you what: Fear is a big waste of time. I'm not afraid of anything."

Beverly threw her baton up high in the air and caught it with a professional snap of her wrist.

Raymie felt her heart clench in disbelief.

"You already know how to twirl a baton," she said.

"So what?" said Beverly.

"Why are you even taking lessons?"

"I guess that is exactly none of your business. Why are you taking lessons?"

"Because I need to win the contest."

"I told you," said Beverly, "there's not going to be a contest. Not if I can help it. I've got all kinds of sabotaging skills. Right now, I'm reading a book on safecracking that was written by a criminal named J. Frederick Murphy. Ever heard of him?"

Raymie shook her head.

"Didn't think so," said Beverly. "My dad gave me

the book. He knows all the criminal ways. I'm teaching myself how to crack a safe."

"Isn't your father a cop?" asked Raymie.

"Yeah," said Beverly. "He is. What's your point? I can already pick a lock. Have you ever picked a lock?"

"No," said Raymie.

"Didn't think so," said Beverly again.

She threw the baton up in the air and caught it in her grubby hand. She made twirling a baton look easy and impossible at the same time.

It was terrible to behold.

Suddenly, everything seemed pointless.

Raymie's plan to bring her father home wasn't much of a plan at all. What was she doing? She didn't know. She was alone, lost, cast adrift.

*I'm sorry I betrayed you.*

*Phhhhtttt.*

*Sabotage.*

"Aren't you afraid that you will get caught?" said Raymie to Beverly.

"I told you already," said Beverly. "I'm not afraid of anything."

"Nothing?" asked Raymie.

"Nothing," said Beverly. She stared at Raymie so hard that her face changed. Her eyes glowed.

"Tell me a secret," whispered Beverly.

"What?" said Raymie.

Beverly looked away from Raymie. She shrugged. She threw the baton up and caught it and then threw it back in the air again. And while the baton was suspended between the sky and the gravel, Beverly said, "I told you to tell me a secret."

Beverly caught the baton. She looked at Raymie.

And who knows why?

Raymie told her.

She said, "My father ran away with a dental hygienist. He left in the middle of the night."

This was not necessarily a secret, but the words were terrible and true and it hurt to say them.

"People are doing that pathetic kind of thing all the time," said Beverly. "Creeping down hallways in the dark with their shoes in their hand, leaving without telling anyone goodbye."

Raymie didn't know if her father had crept down

the hallway with his shoes in his hand, but he had certainly left without telling her goodbye. Considering this fact, she felt a pang of something. What was it? Outrage? Disbelief? Sorrow?

"It makes me really, really mad," said Beverly.

She took her baton and started beating the rubber tip of it into the gravel of the driveway. Small rocks leaped up in the air, desperate to escape Beverly's wrath.

*Wham, wham, wham.*

Beverly beat the gravel, and Raymie looked on in admiration and fear. She had never seen anyone so angry.

There was a lot of dust.

A car painted a brilliant, glittering blue appeared on the horizon and pulled into the driveway and coasted to a stop.

Beverly ignored the car.

She kept beating the gravel.

It didn't look like she intended to stop until she had reduced the whole world to dust.

# *Nine*

"Stop that!" shouted the woman behind the wheel of the car.

Beverly did not stop. She kept whamming away.

"I paid good money for that baton," the woman said to Raymie. "Make her stop."

"Me?" said Raymie.

"Yes, you," said the woman. "Who else is standing here besides you? Get that baton away from her."

The woman had green eye shadow on her eyelids and big, fake eyelashes and also a lot of rouge on her cheeks. But underneath the rouge and the eye shadow and the fake eyelashes, she looked very familiar. She looked like Beverly Tapinski, except older. And angrier. If that was possible.

"Why do I have to do everything?" said the woman.

This was the kind of question that had no answer, the kind of question that adults seemed to be overly fond of asking.

Before Raymie could even attempt some sort of response, the woman was out of the car and had hold of Beverly's baton and was pulling on it and Beverly was pulling back.

More dust rose up in the air.

"Let go," said Beverly.

"You let go," said the woman, who was surely Beverly's mother, even though she wasn't really acting like a mother.

"Stop this nonsense immediately!"

This command issued from Ida Nee, who had appeared out of nowhere and who was standing in front of them with her white boots glowing and her baton stretched out in front of her like a sword. She looked like an avenging angel in a Sunday-school storybook.

Beverly and the woman stopped wrestling.

"What is going on here, Rhonda?" said Ida Nee.

"Nothing," said the woman.

"Can't you control your daughter?" said Ida Nee.

"She started it," said Beverly.

"Get out of here, both of you," said Ida Nee. She pointed her baton at the car. "And don't come back until you can behave properly. You should be ashamed of yourself, Rhonda, a champion twirler like you."

Beverly got in the back of the car, and her mother got in the front. They both slammed their doors at the same time.

"See you tomorrow," said Raymie as the car backed out of the driveway.

"Ha!" said Beverly. "You're never going to see me again."

For some reason, these words felt like a punch to the stomach. They felt like someone sneaking down a hallway in the middle of the night, carrying their shoes in their hand – leaving without saying goodbye.

Raymie turned away from the car and looked at Ida Nee, who shook her head, marched past Raymie, and went into her baton-twirling office (which was really just a garage) and closed the door.

Raymie's soul was not a tent. It was not even a pebble.

Her soul, it seemed, had disappeared entirely.

After a long time, or what seemed like a long time, Raymie's mother arrived.

"How were the lessons?" she asked when Raymie got in the car.

"Complicated," said Raymie.

"Everything is complicated," said her mother. "I can't even begin to imagine why you would want to learn how to twirl a baton. Last summer, it was the lifesaving lessons. This summer, it's twirling. None of it makes any sense to me."

Raymie looked down at the baton in her lap. *I have a plan*, she wanted to say. *And the baton twirling is part of the plan.* She closed her eyes and imagined her father in a booth, in a diner, sitting across from Lee Ann Dickerson.

She imagined her father opening the paper and discovering that she was Little Miss Central Florida Tyre. Wouldn't he be impressed? Wouldn't he want to come home immediately? And wouldn't Lee Ann Dickerson be amazed and jealous?

"What could your father possibly see in that woman?" said Raymie's mother, almost as if she knew what Raymie was thinking. "What could he see in her?"

Raymie added this question to the list of impossible, unanswerable questions that adults seemed inclined to ask her.

She thought about Mr Staphopoulos, her lifesaving coach from the summer before. He was not the kind of man who asked questions that didn't have answers.

Mr Staphopoulos only ever asked one question: "Are you going to be a problem causer or a problem solver?"

And the answer was obvious.

You had to be a problem solver.

Dear Reader,

Here are some facts:

I grew up in a small town in Central Florida.

I competed in the Little Miss Orange Blossom contest.

I did not win.

My father left the family when I was very young.

I missed him; I searched for ways to bring him back.

I can't sing.

I'm not brave.

I tried to do good deeds, and those good deeds often went astray.

I worried about my soul.

I took baton-twirling lessons.

I failed to learn how to twirl a baton.

I made good friends.

Those friends stood with me, beside me, next to me.

They helped me understand that the world is beautiful.

Raymie's story is entirely made up.

Raymie's story is the absolutely true story of my heart.

KATE DiCAMILLO is the *New York Times* bestselling author whose books have been translated into over thirty different languages across the world. She is also a regular winner of awards, most notably the prestigious Newbery Medal, which she won for both *Flora & Ulysses: The Illuminated Adventures* and *The Tale of Despereaux*, which was made into a feature-length animation by Universal Pictures. About *The Magician's Elephant* she says, "I wanted, I needed, I *longed* to tell a story of love and magic. Peter, Adele, the magician, the elephant — all the characters in this book are the result of that longing. I hope that you, the reader, find some love and magic here." Kate lives in Minneapolis, USA.